To Denise –
Thank you for
requesting the novel.
Enjoy!

Drowning in Secret

a novel by

Roger Leslie

Absey & Co.
Spring, Texas

Requests for permission to make copies of any part of the work should be mailed to
Permissions
Absey & Co. Inc.
23011 Northcrest
Spring, TX 77389

Library of Congress Cataloging-in-Publication Data

Leslie, Roger.
  Drowning in secret : a novel / by Roger Leslie.
      p. com.
  ISBN 1-888842-36-9 -- ISBN 1-888842-37-7 (pbk.)
1. Detroit (Mich.)--Fiction. 2. Swimming pools--Fiction. 3. Suburban life--Fiction. I. Title.
  PS3612.E815 D76 2002
  813'.6--dc21

                    2002010260

Designed by Edward E. Wilson

Dedication

*To Ciocia Stas and Ciocia Honey
whose love for life embodies the
indomitable spirit of my ancestry.*

The Secret Sits

We Dance around in a ring and suppose,
But the Secret sits in the middle and knows.

—Robert Frost

Chapter

Whenever his fledgling company faced a setback, Pierce Humphry suffered nightmares of dangling high above churning water. Recently, he scraped his fingers raw clawing the oak headboard that, in his dark dreams, was the crumbling cliff. Above him, a rescuing hand, always out of reach, occasionally tossed him a lifeline that invariably appeared soon after in his waking life. This afternoon, it came as a business deal that resuscitated his lofty dreams and saved his family from financial ruin.

The overhanging cliff of Pierce's nightmare was not nearly as high as he imagined. The Humphrys were not rich. But his expectations for success swelled mountainous-ly, making the distance between his dangling feet and the whitecaps below appear frighteningly vast.

At six o'clock, Pierce sped home tapping his bandaged fingertips against the steering wheel.

I'll let my fingernails grow a little, Pierce decided. He was a man with solutions and exciting news to share. But his announcement would have to wait for another landmark family event: This evening, his son Mark was gradu-ating from the eighth grade.

Checking her chiffon dress in the mirror, June Humphry was pleased that the tan and apricot floral print was still vivid. It helped that, at 38, June maintained a sleek figure. She was proud of her flat stomach and shapely legs. Yet she didn't quite understand why most people thought she was pretty. While others saw sweet green eyes and a narrow mouth that dimpled when she smiled, she felt self-conscious about her porous nose and the flat mole above her lip that she believed totally offset the flow of her fea-tures.

But June felt attractive in this dress, if only because Mark would be so pleased to see her in it. When Mark was little, he suffered his first asthma attack. That night, June held her child, her eldest son, as Pierce raced them to Garden City Hospital. It was a long night. Eventually adrenaline injections left Mark jittery, but restored his breathing.

Afterward, Mark spoke of that night often, sometimes tearfully hugging his mother. He described his relief at see-ing her tan and apricot blur come into focus down the ster-ile hall. When she was by his side, he seemed well again.

That night transformed June. Tired, afraid, relieved, sometimes even pitiful, she nonetheless never felt more alive. Her life had purpose. Faced with the prospect of los-ing her child, she broke through the fear by discovering a new, almost ethereal depth to her maternal instincts.

Oh, she often thought, to hold that sense of myself forever... "The camera!" she remembered and headed to the hall closet to retrieve it.

While letting her hair dry, Nicki slid her diary key from behind the lining of her jewelry box. From the bottom of her dresser drawer, she retrieved the diary and opened it to the first facing. N-I-C-K-I was splashed across both pages. Around her name, she had scribbled hearts and "Ms." and animals ranging from the Divine Child falcon to Pooh bears and angry-eyed snakes coiled around fingers forming a peace sign.

To Nicki the contrast of the V.L.H. embossed denim cover and her art within satisfactorily represented the progress she had made in recreating herself. Her mother had bought her the diary Christmas of 1970 when being Veronica Lynn Humphry was as painful as swallowing wool. So she tossed away the diary until a year later when she began chronicling her life as Nicki.

Though she wouldn't admit it to anyone else, Nicki could confess to her diary how nervous she was about returning to St. Linus for Mark's ceremony. After her own eighth grade graduation there three years ago, Nicki was clench-fisted about burying Veronica and avoiding Fran Davenport, whom Veronica had every reason to loathe.

"Nicki," her mother tapped on the door. "Are you almost ready?"

3

Though she'd written nothing this time, Nicki locked the book with a swift, guilty reflex. "Uh, yeah, just about."

"What are you wearing?"

The delicate rise in her mother's voice annoyed Nicki.

"I'm perfectly capable of dressing myself." Carefully securing her diary and key in their hiding places, Nicki opened her bedroom door. Through the black and white beads hanging in the doorway, she snapped, "Did you iron my shirt?"

June's eyes darted from the messy room to Nicki's heavy make up.

I dare you to comment about either, thought Nicki.

June furled her eyebrows. "I ironed until one o'clock this morning," she said, implying that Nicki would have known if she'd been home by then. "It's hanging with your other blouses in the basement."

"Then I'll be ready in a couple minutes." Nicki closed the door, immediately regretting her curt reply. If only she could admit to her mother how afraid she was to step back into her still-festering past. But when the hall floor creaked, Nicki knew her mother was nearly to the kitchen, too far away for confessions and apologies.

Around the corner from his classmates, Mark stared down the empty corridor of St. Linus School. He stood near the drinking fountain. If anyone rounded the corner he could lean over it as if that were the reason he was here alone. It wasn't. He was ashamed of feeling so afraid. Since he was six years old, this school was all he knew beyond family. Mark had done well here because he was comfortable. He liked the routine of walking to school every morning and leaving each afternoon in single file behind the safety monitor.

Mark clutched the metal gate dividing him now from the corridor of his past. He remembered rubber boots and dripping coats inside the louver lockers, Friday art sessions when Sister Gloria played John Denver albums from her hi-fi, the day his father convinced Miss Porter to let him enter the spelling bee after the deadline because a bout with asthma kept him out of school a week.

"You gonna stand here or get a drink?"

Mark spun toward the water fountain so quickly he shook the metal divide. The clatter pinched his shoulders. Mark took a brief sip then stepped toward the glass door at the opposite side of the hall.

"Why are you over here by yourself?" the student asked, swiping dribble from his lips with his jacket sleeve. "You always do that," he added then disappeared.

Not always, thought Mark.

Only two years ago, seeing his boisterous male classmates become self-conscious around girls made Mark feel mature. He already enjoyed the company of girls. But when they developed attractions to qualities Mark didn't have, he withdrew.

To his dismay, he observed rather than experienced the changing dynamic between his male and female classmates. In their shy, sidelong glances, he sensed a chemistry that he didn't share. If it weren't for his good buddy,

Russell, he would have been entirely alone. Yet even with only one lifeline at this school, Mark was afraid to leave. Each time this fear rose in him, he thought he might cry.

"Mark?"

It was a sweet intonation. He breathed in deeply and hoped his eyes were not red as he turned with a forced smile. It was Beverly Twardowski.

"Why are you over here by yourself?"

"Oh, just thinking." He liked Beverly. She was fun and silly and kind to him.

"It's almost time to start. You ready?"

He wanted to say "yes," but his false enthusiasm might reveal the truth of his fear. Besides, he owed Beverly honesty, for he had first won her compassion by lying to her. In class one day, Mark let his mind wander as students around him eagerly waited to hear who made the football team.

"Why didn't you try out?" Beverly asked.

"The doctor said I can't," he lied, "because of my asthma." Beverly's sympathetic expression made Mark hate himself. She kindly attempted to include him, and he repaid her with a lie. He would not do that again. Ever.

"Are you ready?" she asked again.

Feeling his eyes well, he pounded his hand against his thigh and nodded no.

"I—I'm sure Russell will be here soon."

Mark exhaled nervously. "He's always late, isn't he?"

"Come on," Beverly stroked his arm, "This is our last hour together as a class."

"In a minute."

She hesitated, then stepped around the corner, leaving Mark to compose himself before joining the processional to the church.

In two straight lines, girls left, boys right, the 1974 eighth grade graduating class of St. Linus followed Sister Killeen toward the church. As instructed, Mark stood directly behind the only classmate who repulsed him: effeminate, flamboyant Brian Gillian.

"Mark." From the convent lawn, his mother clicked her Instamatic.

Seeing her floral dress did not comfort as much as the camera embarrassed. Mark wanted to get through this event as inconspicuously as possible. Already she was ruining it.

"Russell," she called and the flash went off again.

When all graduates rearranged themselves alphabetically in the church, Mark ended up in the middle of the second pew. Perfect. Here he didn't need to remember a cue to stand. He could merely stay in sync with the other graduates, walk steadily past Sister Killeen and receive his diploma. He'd approached this altar hundreds of times to take the Eucharist. Even with eyes focused on him, he could do this.

An uncharacteristic summer swelter lingered inside the church. Congregates fanned themselves, dabbed foreheads, rolled their shoulders to free the sweat-soaked polyester blends that clung to their backs. The open windows and ceiling fans whirring too high overhead invited relief but offered none.

Though the full mass extended the time trapped in the

heat, occasionally standing and kneeling kept some guests from falling asleep. In place of the homily the principal gave a speech. Gripping the microphone in her plump hand, Sister Killeen planted herself in the aisle between the graduates.

"In thinking about what I might say to you young people, the idea of beginnings and endings kept surfacing in my mind. For many of you, this is the first time you'll be saying good-bye to what is familiar."

Mark's throat tensed.

"But I have learned through my life experiences that there are no finite beginnings or endings. Life instead is a series of infinite blessings, and even before we let go of old ones, the new have begun to transform our lives for the better. Even in our Lord's ministry, the old laws were making way for His new example years and years before His miracles, and parables, and sermons. Most dramatically, as we recall each Good Friday, what seemed like an end, Jesus' death on the cross, was merely one of many steps toward infinite life with God.

"If we follow the example of Jesus, this graduation marks no end at all. It is a moment in an endless stream of time. Now to you at fourteen, this idea may seem a bit vague. But it is a truth you'll learn many times in your life."

At the back of the church, Pierce fumed, and not because he cradled five-year-old Brandon, who was sweating like a radiator. Pierce seethed because of the sacrilegious outfit Nicki wore as she sat beside him. The gaudy makeup and ridiculous glasses were as ugly as her ragged flared jeans with their glittering patches of snakes and tongues and peace signs. Why Nicki reveled in making him angry, he couldn't understand.

"I will admit," Sister Killeen raised her open palm, "When I walk down the halls of St. Linus next school year, a side of me, the very human side, will notice your absence, remember you fondly, and feel very sad that you're not with me. But the spiritual side, the one blessed by wisdom, will know I'm still holding onto your memory as one segment of my lifelong and even eternal journey toward peace with God.

"As I look around at your bright, expectant faces, I am secretly taking in each smile, feature, mannerism, and I'm keeping them with me." She paused. "Now a piece of you is part of me, and when I feel that fully, I cannot help but express joy. In spirit we're connected forever.

"So no matter where you're heading next year—Divine Child, Catholic Central, Crestwood—you will not be far from home. You can't be, for you take it with you wherever you go."

Mark's woodpecker heartbeat paused every time a flashbulb popped. She never quits, he thought. Then his fingertips checked to make sure the corner of his eyes weren't moist.

"There's no reason then to say good-bye, for you're staying here with me in so many ways. That is the truth, and there's no hiding truth. It shows in everything you do. So instead, as I complete this speech and move back to the altar to assist Father Slaughter in presenting your diplomas, I say simply, 'Congratulations, and farewell.'"

Nicki couldn't remember if Fran's little brother was in Mark's grade, but she would take no chances. Nonchalantly, she scanned the congregation for Fran Davenport. Unlike Veronica, who would have sought Fran out like an anxious child or avoided her like a wounded one, Nicki was no rose petal. In her granny glasses and elephant leg hip-huggers, she was now too cool to be hurt by the likes of Fran Davenport, who, to Nicki's disappointment and relief, was not here.

"Kevin Callahan..." As the first row of graduates approached the platform, June crept forward for a close up of Mark receiving his congratulatory handshake.

Mark didn't see her. The woodpecking accelerated. If he would ever have an anxiety-induced asthma attack, it was now.

Just nerves, he insisted. I'm not frail. I'm no Brian Gillian.

Mark's panic subsided thanks to a strange distraction. Three students down to Mark's left, classmate Gary Mede was sporting a new tan that enhanced his manly features, but accentuated an enormous birthmark on his neck. Mark had seen its vague outline before, but in his childhood naiveté, he thought it was dirt where Gary forgot to wash. Mark stared, simultaneously awed and disgusted that a simple tan could both enhance Gary's physical perfection and pronounce his flaw. The contradiction confounded him.

"Hey!" a sharp whisper and elbow jab caught Mark's attention. "Stand up, stand up." All the students to his right were standing.

"Oh!" Mark sprang to his feet.

One at a time students in his row shuffled to the end of the pew, took the two steps required to reach the chancel, then crossed the sanctuary platform where Sister Killeen waited with extended hand.

"Brian Gillian." He swaggered confidently and shook Sister Killeen's hand with such energy the congregation laughed. He was a showman and had won them over with a mere required handshake.

"Brenda Harrow." Unsteady in high heels, Brenda accidentally kicked the kneeler. It dropped to the down position. Mark was next. He looked at the kneeler.

What do I do? Walk along it? No, too juvenile. I'm next, I'm next. Lean over and raise it? Too much time.

"Mark Humphry."

I'll lift it out of the way with my foot. Yeah, I can do that.

He moved along the pew until it was blocked by the kneeler. From the side? From the front? He couldn't decide so quickly. Clumsily he tried to step behind it. Until this moment he had not realized that his feet were now large as a man's.

When the toe of his shoe kicked the center peg supporting the kneeler, Mark nearly tripped. But he gripped the pew and kept his balance. Finally, Mark stopped, lifted the kneeler out of the way, then moved to the end of the pew.

As he stepped into the aisle, it happened. The outside of his new shoe caught on the last peg of the kneeler and slipped right off his foot. Just as it did, his mother's camera flashed, and someone in the pew behind him laughed. He was sure he heard laughter. He looked down at his upturned shoe and stocking foot.

"Mark?" Sister Killeen prodded jovially to help him save face. "You earned the diploma, we're sure. Come forward."

The congregation chuckled good-naturedly, but Mark was mortified. The seconds it took to flip the shoe upright and slip his foot back in only prolonged his humiliation. All the way to the altar he struggled to work his heel into the shoe and to maintain his composure. It only took Sister Killeen's warm "Congratulations, son" to burst his dam of tears.

He stepped down, his chin buried so deep the knot of his tie choked him. Instead of turning at the second pew to resume his seat, Mark marched right down the side aisle, out the door, and straight toward home.

Chapter

2

Had Mark stayed for the rest of graduation, he would know his little mishap had the impact of a single hiccup. Many congregates didn't even notice the brief delay when he lost his shoe. They either couldn't see that side of the church or weren't paying attention to anyone but their own family member. On the contrary, the innocence of his blunder endeared him to the few parents who saw what happened. Most important, no one saw his tears except Sister Killeen, who searched for Mark afterwards in hopes of hugging the sensitive boy she barely knew before this event.

After the ceremony the graduates mingled on the front lawn of the church. They posed for pictures around St. Linus' statue. They hugged each other, boys and girls, some tearfully.

"How do I know where he is?" June's abruptness stemmed more from concern than mere irritation with Pierce for asking. From their car, the family scanned the church grounds one last time before turning toward home.

"He'll be back," sighed Pierce.

June didn't know Pierce's exact train of thought, but she sensed his undercurrent of judgment for Mark. She was weary of it already.

Go back to being mad at Nicki, she thought, and leave Mark alone.

When he ran from church to the house, Mark swapped his dress clothes for shorts and a T-shirt, then raced his 10-speed to Kinloch Park before his family returned home. Kinloch was not an impressive park by any stretch. It had only one set of swings, some dangling metal rings more dangerous than fun, and a row of concrete stumps along an unfinished parking lot.

At the far end of the park two massive mounds bulged from the earth, tan and dry. The dusty ground around them kept that end of the park in a perpetual gritty fog. From the park entrance, they looked like two giant breasts of a woman nestled beneath the surface. Mark never saw them that way. They were just two dead heaps pressing down on it, heavy, solid, immobile.

There was no obvious reason for their existence. Apparently someone had decided to elevate one side of the park, perhaps for sledding in winter, for the dirt was transported, not dug from anywhere in view. But the idea must have died, and no sign of the plan was left except the two heaps that daredevil children raced over or shy youngsters hid behind to escape the shame of tears.

Mark absently spun the front tire of his bike lying

beside him. He wished he'd brought something: a candy bar, the latest issue of *Rona Barrett's Hollywood*, his paperback of *The Poseidon Adventure*. Just looking at the grainy green headshots on the back cover would help him feel better. A year and a half after he first saw the movie, it still exhilarated him. Instead, he stared at the sky.

A grinding bicycle chain interrupted the silence. "I thought I'd find you here."

Mark closed his eyes. He wasn't ready to see anyone, even his friend, Russell.

"You didn't miss much. Things ended pretty fast after Sister Killeen gave out the diplomas."

Without looking at him, Mark sat up and muttered "hm" to indicate he was listening.

"You did miss one thing. After the graduates all marched out, Father Slaughter pushed Sister Killeen aside. Know what he said?"

Mark didn't recognize Russell's set-up to a favorite line of dialogue from *The Poseidon Adventure*.

"I'm going next so if old fat ass gets stuck in there I won't be caught behind her."

Mark grinned.

Russell continued from another scene. "So...How ya doin', Mrs. Rosen?"

Hesitating momentarily, Mark responded with a shrill Shelley Winters inflection. "Fine, I—I think I'm getting my second wind. Ho—how you dthoing, Mr. Rogo?"

"Fine, fine..." Russell sat beside Mark and dug a crushed pack of Kools from his pocket.

"So," he lit his cigarette then offered one to Mark. "It's

a drag."

"Graduation?"

"No, inhaling a cigarette." His delivery was deadpan. "It's called a drag." He sucked in deeply and let out a huge billow of smoke.

"You're so goofy," Mark chuckled. "What is your problem?"

"I hang around you and you ask me that?"

Silence followed.

"I don't want to talk about it," Mark finally insisted.

"I didn't ask you about it."

"Well don't."

"I wasn't planning to."

"Then change the subject already."

"Okay."

"Okay." The smoke scratched at Mark's constricted throat. Everything was changing so fast.

"I can't stay long," Russell said. "My folks are taking me out to dinner. They just let me go for a few minutes to see that you're all right."

"I'm all right."

"Don't you need to get home?" He stood, flicking his cigarette over the mound. "Bet your mom is worried."

"I don't worry about my mom any more."

"I said she's worried. You don't listen." He mounted his bike. "Let's go."

Mark still didn't want to face his family.

Russell extended his hand and did his best Jack Albertson. "Come on, Belle, it's just a little higher."

Mark had to smile. He dowsed his cigarette and let

Russell help him to his feet. He loved this Shelley Winters-climbing-the-Christmas-tree scene.

"I can't. I can't, Manny. I'm stuck. I'm stuck in the spokes."

"Yes, you can."

Mark hopped on his bike. "I can't, Manny, I can't."

No longer in character, Russell looked directly Mark. "Yes, you can."

They left the park and rode down the block until Russell turned onto his street, leaving Mark to continue home alone.

"He couldn't have gone far on his bike," Pierce insisted, more impatient than worried.

"Oh I know," conceded June. "He's just such a sensitive boy."

She was sitting at her usual place at the kitchen table. With both legs curled at her side, she nervously rubbed her ankle. The table leaf creaked every time she lifted her glass of cream soda.

"Mom."

"What is it, Brandon?"

Though only five, he was cognizant of her curt tone, mostly because she seemed to use it only with him.

"Mom."

"Yes, Brandon!"

"Are we gonna eat that cake?"

A white sheet cake with blue trim and a little plastic

cap and diploma punctuated the rectangular dinner table.

"Not until your brother comes home." June's eyes kept veering toward the glass door where Pierce now stood. Through the open garage door, Pierce had a good view of the driveway. Watching him, June felt a subtle spark ignite within her. It wasn't passion but a familiar old affection. Comfy, she thought, and smiled at the memory.

When they had first met twenty-three years ago, Pierce's bright features and vigor made him so accessible. Even when he tried, he couldn't appear tough. Once he slicked back his hair to look like Marlon Brando in *The Men*, but it was so thick and black he looked instead like Ricky Ricardo. Now he seemed older than his 39 years. Dark circles cupped his eyes, and deep red sores slashed the corners of his mouth.

June was touched to see Pierce watching for Mark so faithfully. Usually consumed with work by day, and frustrated by Nicki's violating curfew at night, he seldom showed such concern for Mark.

"Is he out there?"

Pierce didn't answer at first. "What? Huh?" He turned to her blankly.

"Mark. Do you see him coming?"

"No, no, I just...I think I'll step outside."

June smiled. He was going outside to wait for their son. "Brandon!"

June turned to him as he sucked a huge blue swath of icing from his finger. "What have you—?" One side of the cake was gutted.

"Brandon Paul Humphry, you know better than to—"

"The blue won't come off," he studied his finger. "Will it be blue forever?"

June wrung a dishrag under the tap. "Come here."

"Will it?"

"Will it what?"

"Be blue forever?"

"It's icing, not a tattoo. Of course it won't be blue forever."

She rubbed his tiny finger clean. "Now what are we going to do about this cake?"

"Let's eat it."

"Look, that whole side is ruined. And I didn't get a picture of it yet."

The screen door wheezed.

"Mom." Mark cowered at the threshold.

"Mark!" She rushed forward to hug him, but his sudden stiffness reminded her that they no longer had an intimate rapport. Self-consciously she folded her arms. "I was . . . we were worried."

"Not me," Brandon said, "but I'm glad you're back. I want cake."

"In a minute, son." When June reached Mark, he backed away.

She continued toward the back door and looked out, pretending that was her intent all along. "I'm surprised your father didn't come in with you," she searched the empty driveway. "He's been as worried as I am."

"I didn't mean to ruin things today."

"You didn't ruin anything, son."

Brandon looked up curiously. "Son," he imitated the

stern inflection she used to address him. "Son," he shifted to a tender song meant for Mark. "Son" he furrowed his brow. "Son," he raised it with the pitch of his voice. "Son, son."

"I got some very good pictures...before, when you were marching in."

"I don't want to see them."

"Fine," she snapped, "but you will one day."

Brandon was shocked to hear his mother being stern with Mark.

"Now go wash your face and put your suit back on. I've got two exposures left in the camera and I want pictures of you with your cake."

"I'm tired, Mom. I don't want a picture tonight."

June gasped. Mark had never directly defied her before. She'd always worried that he had no backbone. It seemed unfathomable that he would start exercising his independence against her.

"Then we'll take them in the morning. But I'm getting the pictures."

Mark didn't reply.

"You're tired. Go to bed." She threw open the door and stepped outside.

June didn't find Pierce on their front porch as she expected. Instead she walked out to an empty court. Their house, the middle of nine brick ranch-styles around the circular street, faced the court entrance, blocked only by a cluster of bushes punctuating the grassy island.

"Pierce?" June followed a metallic rattling at the side of the house where they parked their cars. Extending a tape measure across the drive, Pierce surveyed the area so intently he didn't hear June approach. "What are you doing?"

Pierce's chest bulged like a guilty child. "Hi."

"What are you measuring?"

"Oh, just tossing around some ideas."

"You hate carports."

"Carport? No, I don't want a carport. You know me. I'm always building something."

"It's what you do for a living. You don't need to do it at home."

"Ohhhh," he smirked.

June knew the look. He was up to something. Her revived admiration for him fizzled at the pit of her stomach. "When you're done playing out here you've got two sons inside." She left him there.

Nicki was so excited about getting out of the house without facing either her mom or dad, running into him in the driveway stunned her. "Hey."

"Where are you heading?"

"Out." She knew that wouldn't do. "With friends."

"Nelson and Sugar?"

"Her name's Candy."

"Candy. That's a sweet name, too."

Not funny, she thought.

"You work in the morning?"

"Nope." She hopped into her Plymouth Fury.

"Curfew's still the same."

"I know."

"Then meet it this time."

She slammed her door and roared around the court on her way to Toke's apartment.

Knowing Toke gave Nicki a secret life apart from home and school. He first came into Manufacturers Bank that spring carrying a motorcycle helmet and wearing an earring shaped like a metal washer. After hello, he rattled off his huge plans for getting rich then segued into inviting her to a Santana concert at Pine Knob. Waiting for her answer, he grinned expectantly as if unashamed of the gap between his teeth.

"All right."

From the start, Nicki made assumptions about Toke that all proved wrong. Because he drove a Harley and had the posture of a buffalo, she figured he was insensitive. But at the outdoor concert, he noted her discomfort as he pulled out a bag of weed, and immediately put it away.

When he invited her to his apartment, she assumed he wanted sex. Turned out he only wanted to show her his collection. Knowing he smoked pot and made irregular banks deposits, Nicki anticipated an array of drug paraphernalia. Instead, he pulled out jewelry hand-crafted out of hardware. He showed her nails twisted into rings, metal bracelets with cabinet knobs welded all around, and earrings made from mollies.

"Can you paint?" he asked.

"Paint?"

"Yeah. I don't have a good eye for color. I'm gonna

carve designs into some pieces, and I'll need 'em painted. You game?"

Nicki said yes before wondering what was in it for her. From then on, instead of going out, they usually ordered in pizza or picked up 7-in-a-bag-for-a-buck from White Castle and crafted jewelry in his apartment. With Bowie or Rod or Yes blaring, they worked, drank a little too much, and ended up snuggling on the couch.

Tonight, it was 7 and 7 and Ziggy Stardust. Slumped side-by-side on the plaid sofa, Toke leaned over and kissed her. Nicki closed her eyes and imagined it was her friend Nelson, who wasn't hairy or burly or forward like Toke. He also wasn't interested in her.

Before Toke got too carried away, she pulled back. His groggy compliance relieved her guilt for drinking his liquor, eating on his dime, then not giving him what he wanted.

"Should I leave?"

"Nah," he groaned. "I'm just glad you're here." Then he slipped his arm under her head and held her close until they both nodded off.

With the boys in bed and Pierce still outside, June re-entered the quiet kitchen. "Tsk. My beautiful cake." The exposed gash was already hardening.

I better take a picture of it tonight, she thought, hope for rescuing this disastrous day reviving in her again. "I can still get a good a shot or two." She dabbed the Sylvania

Blue Dot with her tongue and snapped it onto the camera. Her first view through the lens was unimpressive. The blue and white cake blended nauseatingly into the turquoise tablecloth. She set aside the camera and arranged various linen napkins around the cake. She hated them all, especially the way the red Christmas ones combined with the blue and white like Pierce's American Company logo.

When the napkins didn't work, she brought linens from the hall closet, finally settling on a periwinkle sheet. She bunched it beneath the cake then punctuated the camera shot with silver candlesticks. "Now that's worthy of a picture."

June held the camera steady. When she depressed the shutter release, nothing happened.

"Hm." She rotated the advance wheel, but it didn't move. "That's odd." Replacing the flashcube at a different angle didn't help either. The picture still wouldn't take.
"What the—?" She checked the back of the camera to see how many exposures were left. The little window was empty. Her film was gone.

That's impossible, she thought. After I took the last shot at church, I had two exposures left.

June rummaged through the camera case, tossing out an unopened box of film, the camera strap she never used, flash cubes. No used cartridge.

Rifling through stacks on the kitchen junk table and clothes in her bedroom drawers, June mentally traced the exposures on the roll of film back to Easter. On her hands and knees she skimmed her closet floor. She even rubbed her hands up and down the garment bag protecting the

24

dress she'd worn. It wasn't there either.

"What are you looking for?" Pierce asked.

"Oh, you scared me. I didn't hear you come back in."

"What did you lose?"

"I didn't lose anything. The film is missing from the camera."

"I didn't take it."

"God, you're like one of the kids! I didn't accuse you, I simply answered your question." She wished he'd just stayed outside and out of her way.

"You're gonna be up all night looking for it, I suppose. Might as well. I'll be up pacing till Nicki gets home any- how."

"I told you," June insisted, "Take the car away from her. How else—?" She stopped. He knew the rest. "Do what you want about that. You will anyway. I'm busy." Then she scoured the car and every room the camera or case could possibly have been that day. When it didn't turn up, she searched again, retracing every step from getting dressed for graduation to waiting for Mark's return. Finally spent, June decided to resume her search the next morning by questioning the boys.

While getting ready for bed, June still fixated on the cartridge. As she wiped off her makeup at the bathroom sink, a thought pierced through her. "No," she dismissed it. "Mark wouldn't do that."

My old Mark wouldn't, she thought. But he was chang- ing.

The Noxema stung June's cheeks. She washed her face, dabbed it with astringent, and pitched the used cotton balls into the waste pail.

From the corner of her eye she noticed something black beneath the white tissues in the pail. When she bent down to get a better look, she knew immediately what it was—the film cartridge. Excitedly she reached for it, but grabbed only one rounded end. Digging past the cotton and tissues, June found the rest of the cartridge. It was smashed to bits. Tangled around the fragments was the unfinished roll of film, exposed, ruined.

She didn't want to believe it, but the evidence was in her hand. Mark hurt her in the cruelest way possible. He destroyed her memories.

It had been such an emotionally charged day, Pierce probably would have had trouble sleeping anyway. But tonight he particularly resented waiting up for Nicki. All evening he'd anticipated sharing his big news with the entire family. Instead, tonight was like too many others. With the boys oblivious to it all, June in a stew about something, and Nicki out past her curfew, Pierce was left to watch the clock and percolate with every passing second.

What does she do out this late? Pierce worried. When unbearable possibilities flashed through his mind, he returned to wondering how Nicki went from adoring him to resenting him.

If I could just figure it out, he believed, I could make life the way it was before. As long as she continues defying me, I've got to discipline her. But what haven't I tried? I've talked to her, grounded her, even threatened to follow her. I only dig the cavern between us deeper.

More than once, June suggested that he take away Nicki's car. But he and Nicki had made a deal when they bought her Fury: He'd co-sign the note and cover her insurance, but if she made the payments, it was her car. In honoring their agreement, Nicki demonstrated integrity. He didn't want to take that away from her.

At 12:30, Pierce heard Nicki pull into the drive. He moved to his usual spot at the end of the foyer and tightened the belt of his robe.

She stepped through the front door and waited. Their mutual silence told Pierce they had reached an impasse. He had no more punishments to mete out, she was clearly not wasting breath with explanations. He shook his head with a scowl, and left her standing in the hall alone.

Chapter

3

Pierce sprang out of bed the next morning determined to share his big news. "Hon, get up. I've got something exiting to tell everybody."

Throwing on his robe, he raced to Nicki's room. He didn't care how tired she was. "Nicki," he banged on her door. "I have big news for us all. Get up."

"Boys," he shouted before reaching their room. "Mark and Brandon, I've got a surprise that you'll love."

The family gathered in the kitchen where Pierce waited, a strangely giddy grin tightening his jowls. Only Brandon could meet Pierce's energy so early in the morning. "What's my surprise?"

"I closed a deal yesterday—"

Before his sentence ended, June leered.

Pierce noticed, but dismissed it. "What is it we've talked about getting so long?" He looked at Brandon for a reply.

"A snowmobile?"

"Brandon, it's summer, son. What are we going to do

with a snowmobile? No."

"Well, we wanted one."

"You're right, we did. But, no, this is the greatest thing we could get for the summertime."

"Just tell us," June grumbled.

Pierce looked at her, wounded. "This is important. To all of us."

"Then what is it?"

It would have been so easy to shout, "Damn it, can't you just be supportive for once? This is for you!" But this announcement was too important. Pierce wanted to share it the right way. He took a deep breath and grazed his bandaged forefinger along the ulcerous sore at his mouth.

"Dad, you upset?"

"No, Brandon. Frustrated."

"What did I do?"

"Nothing," he pulled Brandon toward him. "I just wanted to tell everybody that we're putting in a pool."

"What?"

"That's the big news."

"A pool?" He had captured Nicki's attention, who to this point would not look at him.

"Yes," Pierce's excitement revived, "a pool!"

"A five-footer?"

"Five foot? No," he realized now what Nicki was thinking. "No, no, not an above-ground pool. I'm talking built-in pool."

"Where?"

"In our back yard. We are going to be the first family in Dearborn Heights to have a built-in pool of our own."

"Won't that be expensive?" asked June.

"Don't you worry, Hon."

"I thought we were cutting back?"

"This won't change our household budget a dime. Promise. Well, what do you think?"

"Will I have to wear a life jacket every time I go in?"

"Brandon, you'll be such a good swimmer by the end of the summer we won't be able to get you out until it starts to freeze over."

"Really?"

Pierce felt the atmosphere of the room shifting. Brandon's and Mark's eyes met; their individual exhilaration melded and lit their faces. Even June's posture opened. It was finally happening. Pierce had them on his side. For the first time in so long they were acting like a family.

Brandon pelted his father with a barrage of questions. "Will it be like at the Holiday Inn? Will it have a diving board? I want a slide. Can we get a slide?"

"Brandon!" June erupted. "Let your father tell us about—" She swallowed and completed her thought more gently, "about his new plans... for all of us."

Pierce smiled at June gratefully. "It will be kidney shaped."

"Like a kidney bean?" Mark hopped onto the counter.

"No, like, like," Pierce imagined an aerial shot of the pool. "Like a fish without fins."

"What?" Brandon's brows met.

"Like a diamond?" Mark asked, sliding open the drawer with his thumbs and slamming it shut with his dangling calf.

"Not exactly."

"Oval?" Nicki offered.

"No. Not oval."

"Like paisley," said June.

"Yes, like paisley."

"What's that?" asked Brandon.

Mark was still fidgeting with the drawer. "Remember the blue and gray dress Mom wore to midnight mass last Christmas?"

"No."

Nicki snarled at Mark. "You are so weird."

"Remember she wore it in that picture Dad took of her in front of the hall mirror?"

Brandon stared blankly.

"Like a Spirograph design, but stretched long. Right?"

June grabbed the front of the drawer at Mark's legs. "Stop that banging."

From the open drawer filled with plastic holiday placemats, Mark pulled out a Thanksgiving mat and pointed to a cornucopia.

"Like this, Brandon," his father grabbed the mat and covered the narrow end with his hand. "Lop off this side and close off the opening and there you have it."

"Like that?"

"Yes."

"Where do you put the diving board?"

"I don't know yet, son. We haven't finished the design."

"Design?" June wondered. "If you're buying a real pool, what would you have to do with the design?"

Ignoring June's question, Pierce held up the placemat like a flag. "That's what our pool's going to look like."

"Our pool," June mumbled, but no one seemed to hear her.

In the privacy of her room Nicki expressed excitement to the only family member she trusted: her diary. No mere book, it was her secret sister. With an uptight father, a mom who was June Cleaver on her period, and two brothers who showed no sign of attaining her level of cool, Nicki created a family comrade to make bearable her dreary middle class life in the suburbs.

Nicki had struggled to choose just the right persona for her diary. Since no one in real life impressed her, she sought a fictional character who embodied how she felt. With little interest in literature, Nicki couldn't remember many books, let alone characters. But she did recall being impressed by one unit in freshman English: mythology. Stories of grand supernatural beings that embodied whole elements of life and nature fascinated her, especially one invincible goddess.

What was her name? Nicki had strained to recall details. Goddess of war and wisdom, she fought a lot, even winning a victory over one of the most powerful gods, whose name right now also eluded her.

Somewhere I still have that *Mythology* book, thought Nicki.

Too hard to find in the war zone of her bedroom, she

decided to simply remember the goddess' name. Hera? No, Hera was married to Zeus, and this goddess sprang from Zeus's head. Yeah, Zeus was her father. He had a terrible headache one day, then out she popped. She was not conceived physically but mentally. "Bomb!"

What was her name? Alena. Alena? Lena? That sounded close. Aletha? No, that's not it. Leda. Leda? Yeah, maybe. Leda. Satisfied it could be right, Nicki christened her diary Leda, her own Greek goddess and only true confidant.

> *Leda,*
>
> *I'm getting a built-in pool. Maybe now I have a reason to stay home. That would probably keep Dad off my back. Ah, what a relief not to be hounded and pestered each time I walk through the door.*
>
> *Doesn't he get it? The more rotten he is to me for coming home late, the harder it is for me to come home at all.*
>
> *I think he's a fool for staying up and worrying. It's not like I'm out doing the nasty. I bet he thinks I am, though. Good. Let him think it. If he's not gonna trust me, then anything he makes up in his head he deserves.*
>
> *Oh, back to the pool. I can work on my tan now. And I think I'll go to Hudson's and buy a new bikini even before the pool's put in. Hard to believe, Leda, but Dad says it'll only take a couple weeks to dig it and have it ready.*
>
> *Maybe I'll have a pool party on the 4th. Yeah, I*

can buy a red and white striped bikini and find some shades in the shape of blue stars. Cool. I bet Toke'd know where to get shades like that.

Toke's the bomb. Sometimes I feel bad about never giving him anything, especially what I think he wants — you know, sexually. But then the other day he asked if I wouldn't mind going to Duke's Hardware and picking up some new pieces for making jewelry. He tried to pay me back, but I wouldn't let him. Hell, it was only about five dollars. I figure it's the least I could do.

I'm partying with Nelson and Candy tonight — Hines Drive, of course.

Later,

N

When Nicki stopped writing, her diary flipped back to an earlier entry. Nicki's heart froze. The page had a tear in it.

My diary! she thought. The one perfect, secret portion of her life was damaged.

But her second thought shot crystallized impulses through her: She never remembered tearing the page. If she had, even by accident, she'd have heard it rip. The only other explanation seemed impossible. How could anyone have found Leda? Even if they did, they couldn't open her without the key. While an ounce of suspicion dripped from her icy veins, Nicki told herself there was just no way. She had hidden the book and key too well.

I musta done it myself, she concluded. "Sorry, Leda,

didn't mean to," she told her diary. But as she put her away, paying close attention to how delicately she handled her secret friend, a puddle of anxiety formed in the pit of her stomach.

June sat across the kitchen table from Mark thinking about her ruined film. "I didn't see Russell's parents in the church at graduation. Surely they wouldn't have missed it."

"No, they were there," Mark offered casually between bites of Count Chocula.

"I thought I'd see his mother snapping pictures with me."

"I don't know if she takes a lot of pictures. I've only been in their house a couple times. I don't even remember if they have many pictures on the wall."

"Not like us," June turned off the burner when her tea kettle whistled. "We love pictures."

"Um-hm," Mark agreed. "I don't know anybody who takes more pictures than you."

June poured the hot water. "I wonder how those shots I took of you heading to the church will come out?" She dunked her tea bag and waited for Mark's reaction.

"I'm sorry," Mark said.

With her back to him, June smiled.

"I just screwed up the thing so bad."

The thing? Did he mean the film? "Watch your language, son," was all she said.

"Oh, sorry. I just…we stood up…the kneeler fell…I couldn't think that fast …bend down? Step over it?"

June returned to her seat. "It happened. It's over."

Tears Mark struggled to fight back appeared anyway.

"Mark, don't cry. What if your brother or sister walked in?"

He blew his nose into his napkin.

"You know right from wrong. If you've done something you feel guilty about…?" She wondered at Mark's perplexed expression.

"Guilty? I tripped."

"Not that, Mark. Course I know you tripped. Everybody in the church saw that!"

With a nervous timbre, Mark burst into laughter.

"What?" June smiled. "What's so funny?"

"I tripped in church. It wasn't a mortal sin."

She began laughing now, too.

"It's a good thing I broke my fall. Maybe if I hit the ground you'd'a had me incarsonated."

"Incarson—? Mark," they laughed together. "It's incarcerated, not incarsonated."

Mark roared even louder. "I know that word. I meant incarsonated. You haven't heard of that prison? For punishment you gotta stay up and watch Johnny Carson every night."

"I like Johnny Carson."

"So do the prisoners. That's why they make the death row inmates watch Merv Griffin."

This was the old Mark she loved. His confession could wait. Until then, she wanted to still time and savor this moment with her son.

Chapter

4

In the dawn hours of June 17th, less than two weeks after Pierce's announcement, N. Bankle Court awoke to the sound of front end loaders, concrete mixers, and five-yard dumps. Some neighbors stepped onto their porch to check out the clamor. Others came out to get their newspaper, then watched as one-by-one trucks strained to cut the turn up the Humphry's drive. Even neighbors who seldom stirred till 9:00 peered curiously out their windows.

In his bedroom, Mark snapped up the vinyl shade just as the front end loader pulled in, its tracks devouring a huge swath of grass. The truck forged toward the back yard, every slab of the driveway cracking and popping under its weight. When the truck disappeared from view, it left behind a small mountain range of broken cement.

Dad'll be furious, Mark pictured his father's worry lines bulging red. But Mom! The noisy trucks would upset her. She'll hate the changes and resent the attention they drew from the neighbors.

Imagining her frustration, Mark pulled the quilt over

his head. A cool rush of air breathed across his exposed feet. He looked down where the quilt used to cover them completely. Veins wrapped around his curved insteps, and tufts of hair darkened his thick, uniform toes. His were the sturdy feet of a man.

Quickly, Mark hid them under his quilt. It wasn't because they were cold. They couldn't be. Mark had woken to the heat of summer.

Flying from Detroit to Chicago with a connecting flight to Oshkosh, Pierce missed the groundbreaking of the pool. Buckled into his aisle seat, he paused to imagine the trucks approaching his driveway. His heart expanded from the fulfillment of a dream born on the fateful day he met the great Henry Ford himself.

Enrolled at Henry Ford Trade School in a program for underprivileged boys, William Pierce Humphry was working at a steel lathe when rumblings of Henry Ford's arrival sent managers scrambling to pick up debris from the aisles. Metal bolts, scraps of steel, pieces of rubber tubing flew into bins like gnats at a fruit market. Employees interrupted their work to blow away soot and shavings from their stations. They tucked in their shirt tails, wiped grease from their anxious faces.

William had been terrified of Henry Ford all his life. When he was a toddler, William was scolded for climbing onto the spare tire encasement of his wealthy aunt's Lincoln Continental. He didn't remember the punishment, but he could still hear the word "Ford" coming from his mother's angry lips. Who was this giant? wondered little William Pierce. Why did he mean so much to his family? William knew only one person who didn't love Henry Ford—his Uncle Jack. But he'd shamed the family with two unforgivable sins: He was a drunk, and he didn't work for Ford.

William's fear escalated as Ford neared. Above the mechanical din, William listened for footsteps. The micrometer jiggled in his trembling hand as he imagined a towering, long-haired Samson approaching. That image shattered when the factory manager turned the corner with a thin, well-dressed man. No taller than any of William's uncles or teachers, he wasn't intense but staid.

Until the manager spoke, William thought Henry Ford hadn't come at all, but had sent a skinny underling in his place. "Mr. Ford, this is one of our top students and perhaps the hardest working young man I know, William Pierce Humphry."

Too nervous to meet the slender man's eyes, William stared at the hairs peeking under his felt hat.

"William, meet Mr. Henry Ford."

William muttered, "I'm pleased to me you, sir."

When Ford shook his moist hand, William was awed by the great man's grip.

"This is your work, son?" Ford asked, inspecting a bearing William had nearly completed.

"Yes, sir. By the time I'm done, I'll have the entire axle completed myself."

"In near record time, I might add." The manager

smiled.

"Very impressive work. I'm proud to have you as part of my team."

With a single compliment, Ford was no longer the unapproachable giant who ran the world, but just a guy who made dreams reality. Pierce, as he now insisted on being called, immediately began nurturing big dreams of his own. He excelled at the trade school, developing his drafting skills so quickly that teachers recommended him for an architect job at Detroit Oil. There, several quick promotions convinced Pierce that greater success was inevitable.

Exposed to life's finer elements at dinner meetings and conferences, Pierce grew impatient. Moderate success wasn't enough. He wanted to be first and best at everything.

He was proud of his new Lincoln Continental until he realized that his aunt was younger than he when she bought hers. So he taught June to drive and bought her a little white Valiant. They became the first two-car family among all his relatives.

While June was pregnant with Mark, Pierce moved the family to a three-bedroom red brick house on N. Bankle. Though nothing extraordinary, it was a solidly built home with a big back yard. Imagining the pool construction in that yard now, Pierce felt his limited past converging toward an unprecedented future.

But he couldn't savor his distraction long. On his lap were so many Union stipulations their bulk tore the clasps of his vinyl briefcase. He couldn't understand why they continued to worry him so. The toughest job was behind him. He negotiated a tripartite agreement with the Detroit Unions to let The Morgan Company build his hotel bathroom modules in their Oshkosh plant. It was unprecedented, but Pierce secured the Union's permission so long as a Union man worked on every step of production.

Especially today, Pierce wished his struggling American Company could afford to keep someone in Oshkosh full time to oversee all module construction. He knew how single-minded both Union men and factory workers could be. He hated being at their mercy, but what could he do? Except for his secretary, his poor gopher Ed Mandusky, and a crew that was now otherwise engaged, Pierce was on his own. So every other week, he flew to Oshkosh to check on the progress of the modules, and to ensure that the Union contract was being honored to the letter.

This long distance setup immobilized him like a struggling wrestler pressed against the canvas. But Pierce couldn't afford to build the modules without The Morgan Company's backing, so it had to be Oshkosh. Thank God this was temporary. Now that Holiday Inn was interested in using the modules for their national expansion, he was about to be a very rich man.

Taking his first sip of Cutty and water, Pierce surveyed the cabin. Through the half-drawn curtain dividing him from first class, a slender stewardess served cocktails.

Usually, Pierce would have felt a rich flutter of attraction for her sleek legs. Today, he looked past them and envied the expansive space at the first class businessmen's feet. Instead of admiring how delicately she passed a tiny bottle of Chevas Regal, Pierce contrasted the rich gold and burgundy emblem with the gaudy yellow Cutty Sark label in hand.

His big moment in life was so near that his feet tingled, anxious to burst out of an impatient paralysis that nothing stimulated except more work. He set aside his drink, opened his briefcase and reviewed the hard-line Union wording again.

Though Brandon was only five, even he could predict Mom's reaction to the damaged driveway. She'd throw a fit, curse in Polish like Babka used to, then be mad at him, or Mark, or Nicki—maybe all of them until Dad got home. Then she'd tell Dad all about it and make everything seem Dad's fault, which it always was, until he fixed everything, which he always did.

Since she would be mad anyway, Brandon saw no reason to miss an opportunity to race his Matchbox cars up and down the great new driveway collision course. He grabbed his cars from the garage toy box, determined to play in the destruction until his mother caught him and forced him to stop.

"Hey."

The voice startled him. Then he realized it was just a neighbor girl, Sao Nerus. "Hey, what?"

Sao was eating a peanut butter and jelly sandwich. She bit into the middle of one side and worked straight through the center. "What are they doing back there?"

"Puttin' in a pool."

"Then what are they digging for?"

"They're not diggin' for nothin'. They're puttin' in the pool."

"Can we go swimming?"

"The pool ain't even in yet."

Sao looked at Brandon incredulously. "I didn't mean now."

"Oh, I guess. I don't know."

"Will you ask your mom?"

"Now?"

"I have a bathing suit, you know. We went to the lake last month and I got a new one."

Brandon looked up indifferently. By this time Sao had made her way through the center of the sandwich. Crumb-speckled lines of tan and purple extended from her mouth to her ears. "Well?" she asked.

"You wanna play cars?"

Sao knelt beside him excitedly.

"Not just mine. Get yours, too."

"Oh," and Sao ran toward her house, teeth-indented quarter moons of sandwich in each hand.

Still lying on the top trundle bed, Mark looked out the window and wondered why Brandon would doom himself to their mother's wrath. If Brandon were its only casualty, Mark wouldn't care. But after scolding Brandon, she'd turn to Mark, call him "my little helper" or something equally demeaning, then give him a list of chores.

He used to like helping her. But now, doing things for her, and especially with her, embarrassed him. Just last month he felt ashamed when the neighbor kids saw them hosing down the storm windows together. He knew the feeling wasn't fair. She didn't do anything wrong. But it was there, and it bothered him.

When they were alone, he enjoyed her company. Even now as he walked into the kitchen, he was disappointed that she wasn't in her usual place at the table.

Mark knew her absence meant only one thing: Angry over the pool's disruption of their lives, she was still in bed. As he ate his Lucky Charms, Mark traced his mother's day, imagining how her mood would darken the household. She would awake around 10:00, sullen and preoccupied. Instead of saying whole sentences about it, she would snap out little comments from a stockpiled arsenal she'd use against Dad when he got home.

I'm spending today outside, he decided. Russell was coming by at noon. Watching the construction crews could fill a good bit of their day.

As he finished eating, Mark heard the screech of pipes. The house was usually so quiet he could distinguish every noise. At each end of the short hall between the turquoise kitchen and the faded green bedrooms, the floor creaked from the slightest weight. In the basement, the hot water heater "bloop"ed like an alien from *Lost in Space*. If the plumbing screeched, it was the outside spigot on the wall beside him.

Brandon's up to no good, Mark thought. He flung

aside the kitchen curtains and curled his fist to knock on the window. He stopped short. Not seeing Brandon's blond head literally took Mark back a step and left him staring through the sheer curtain. What he saw seemed so out-of-place it was disorienting. In the background, a D-4 Cat was tearing off the top layer of earth and building a small mountain of black and green sod. Nearby men in yellow hard hats and rolled up sleeves peered through measuring rods and marked off sections of the yard with string.

In the foreground of this activity crouched his mother. Seemingly unfazed by the chaos around her, she doused a rag and wrung it out. Moving to the clothes lines a few feet beside her, she wrapped the damp towel around each nylon line and marched back and forth between the poles wiping them clean. In one sweeping motion, she flung damp sheets over her shoulder and spaced them out neatly until the lines sagged from the weight of clean, wet bedding.

When Mark couldn't find any defiance in his mother's expression, he looked for it in her actions. There was none. She methodically pulled wooden clothespins from her apron pocket, secured one sheet, then repeated the motion for the next.

It's nine o'clock in the morning, thought Mark. To have washed a basket full of clothes by now meant Mom must have been up by at least 7:30 or 8:00.

His heart landed in his stomach and brought up the marshmallow sweetness of his cereal. But wonder filled Mark as he watched.

When the roar of the front end loader sputtered and

died, the crew foreman, Frank Willis, waved from around the hill of upturned grass. "Morning, Mrs. Humphry. Looks like we both got an early start."

Her eyes sparkled as from a dream. "It's the kind of day I just have to hang out clothes. It'll be breezy, don't you think?"

"Yeah."

"I won't be in your way, will I?"

"Oh, no."

"If you boys get hot out here, we've got plenty of pop in the fridge. Pierce and I stocked up on Faygo because we were expecting you. Just knock on the back door and I'll have one of the kids get you some."

Though Mark was flabbergasted, a smile spread across his face. *Maybe Dad's pool will start something good after all.*

Just before Russell was to arrive, Mark put on a T-shirt and pair of shorts. Ah! No white shirt, gray necktie with the burgundy S.L.S. emblem, and best of all, no black dress shoes. Finally, the barefoot days of summer. But as he stepped outside, Mark looked down at his feet and felt suddenly shy. He returned to his room and pulled on his Keds hightops. Though a little snug, they were warm and, in their own way, comfortable.

When Mark returned to the porch, Russell had already left his old Schwinn Heavy Duty at the curb and was making his way up the broken drive. "Why is your mom hanging out clothes when those construction guys are tearing up your yard?"

"The weather's nice?" Mark shrugged.

"Oh." Although he wore good clothes even to play, Russell was permanently disheveled. His white shirt and black slacks always looked slept in. Beneath his loose shirttail, baby fat hung over his hips. He looked at the driveway. "Do these guys know what they're doing?"

"Let's see." Mark led Russell to the backyard to watch the digging crew. Brandon and Sao were already playing on a mound, clumps of burnt red clay sticking to their sweaty hair.

"How big is it going to be?" Russell shouted over the roar of machinery.

Mark shrugged. "It'll be nine feet deep, I know that." Despite his father's painstaking attempt to explain it, Mark couldn't remember if he said it was kidney or liver shaped (he knew it was one of those organs). He was not about to describe it as paisley. Instead of making a mistake, he'd offer that information after he got it right.

From the far side of the house, his mother's voice rose above the clatter. "You boys stay out of their way, now. I don't want anybody getting hurt. Brandon, what are you doing there? You and Sao keep away from the men. Mark, watch your brother."

If they were younger, Mark and Russell would play in the mess like Brandon. Now getting dirty appealed to neither of them. After a few minutes, watching it wasn't even that exciting.

"You want to find something to do?" Mark moved toward the house, Russell right behind him.

On the front porch they stared at each other without a word. Finally Russell blurted in his bawdiest Stella Stevens inflection, "Will you shut up?!"

Both boys laughed, as if this weren't the hundredth time they'd said that line.

It was just after Christmas of '72 that Pierce took the family to see *The Poseidon Adventure*. It impacted Mark like no other film. He loved everything about it: the capsization, the dramatic deaths, the underwater rescue. But more than any individual scene was the incredible upside down world itself. Because Mark always loved to climb, he was enthralled watching the cast journey up the Christmas tree and staircase, through ducts, up shafts and across catwalks. Though most reviews that Mark read panned the stereotypic characters, he liked the idea of strangers working together to survive. This movie was his ultimate fantasy.

Mark's fascination inspired him to learn everything about the film and to see it as many times as his parents would allow. Unwisely Mark talked too much about the movie to his mother, whose tolerance for others' interests thrived like cut flowers. When she said it wasn't good for him to see any movie too much, Mark knew what she really meant. She was sick of hearing him talk about it.

Curbing his enthusiasm for *Poseidon* at home only intensified it with Russell. Soon they were both avid fans. Though they were permitted to see it only twice, Mark's scheming got them in a third time during the film's first run. One afternoon June took them to Wonderland Mall where they convinced her to let them shop on their own for two hours. Out of range from her suspicious glare, they raced across Plymouth Road to the Terrace Theater. Fumbling in the dark, they found two seats just as the ship's nurse demonstrated in embarrassment what to do with a suppository. It was one of several favorite moments that Mark and Russell still imitated.

In spring of 1974, a commercial advertising *The Poseidon Adventure*'s re-release revved Mark for another viewing. With permission and a ride from Pierce, Mark and Russell were in line outside the Dearborn Theater a half hour before the new run's first showing.

"Why are you wearing a coat?" Russell asked. "It's warm out here."

"I came prepared," said Mark as they approached the ticket booth. "Tell you later." Once seated in the dark, Mark pulled a tape recorder from under his jacket.

"What is it? I can't see." When the previews started, Russell saw the microphone glisten.

"I'm gonna get the whole thing," Mark whispered.

While impressed by Mark's ingenuity, Russell was dismayed that Mark didn't include him in the plan. For the first time Russell realized that Mark could keep secrets, even from him.

It rained most of that spring. They spent the soggy days in Mark's garage listening to the tapes and memorizing the lines. Their best moments were the Gene Hackman/Ernest Borgnine arguments because those were the only roles they never fought over. Mark wanted to be Hackman because he was the hero; Russell insisted on Borgnine because, of the major stars, he was the only survivor.

The Poseidon Adventure's box office momentum kept it in theaters, and eventually drive-ins, all the way into summer. Even now, it was at the Dearborn Drive-in. Mark couldn't wait to catch another showing.

"You know when the pool is finished we can do the underwater scenes," Mark offered as they hopped on their bikes and headed to Kinloch Park.

"Yeah!" Russell beamed. "And you know why?"

"Why?"

Russell cleared his throat. "'Cause 'this is no god damn engine room!'"

Without missing a beat, Mark responded with the Stella Stevens line that followed. "Then where the hell are we?"

"There was a corridor here leading to the engine room. I went through it."

"But now it's underwater."

"So we'll swim through it. It couldn't be more than thirty-five feet at the most."

"Oh is that all?!"

Laughing about Mark's exaggerated inflection, they sped around the court en route to Kinloch Park.

The brisk activity of the Oshkosh plant rivaled Pierce's own excited mind. Weaving past nine foot tall boxes ready to be shipped and around the rough framing stations where modules rolled toward the testing area, Pierce smiled or shook hands with nearly every man along the way. In this environment Pierce felt triumphant. Here he was in his element. He saw himself as a celebrity, a successful young executive in a charcoal gray Brooks Brothers suit walking past men, nearly all older than he, who were still doing for a living what Pierce did back in trade school. While he didn't feel superior to these men, he did feel distinct from them, noticeably commanding respect by the confidence of his gait and the warmth of his acknowledgments.

He stopped at a finishing station to admire the work of a young tradesman installing ceramic tiles around the tub.

"This is a fine job, young man."

Instantly Pierce was Henry Ford, reliving the same encounter he'd had as the awestruck apprentice 25 years ago. Pierce smiled, exploring how this exchange felt from the other side.

The young worker looked more confused than awed. "Do I know you?" was all he asked before resuming his task.

Pierce grinned bravely. He wouldn't let the opportunity to relive this precious memory be diminished by an insult.

"Not yet, but in about a month..." and he pressed on through the labyrinth of men and machines.

Arriving at the Model T's, so named by his secretary as a clever euphemism for the less than impressive "toilet," Pierce stood riveted by his own innovation. Each 8' x 14' x 9' pre-assembled bathroom module was complete and ready to be installed into the frame of any superstructure.

With only the loose pipes to be connected after installation, the modules stood as fully painted, papered and accessorized bathrooms. The chrome hardware shimmered in the intense overhead lights. The new tiles glistened around the tub. Even the light fixtures beside the mirror twinkled.

Plant manager Howard Creep approached.

"Howard, how is everything going?"

"You see them. What do you think?"

Pierce ignored Howard's belligerence. "They look great. You're doing fine work." He surveyed the job, noticing every detail, including the Union label affixed to the plumbing tree.

"Everything working out all right with the Union guys we've contracted out to you?"

"We're all doin' our jobs. Can't ask for more'n that."

"No," Pierce was growing weary of Howard's antagonism. "Thanks again, Howard. These are coming together beautifully."

Then Pierce left the factory wishing this work were being done closer to home.

Long ago Mark and Russell chose Kinloch Park as their hangout. Russell never questioned Mark's insistence that they go to the least impressive park in Dearborn Heights. He had no way of knowing that Mark's decision was less an endorsement of Kinloch than avoidance of Riverside. Even six years after that humiliating spring, Mark still never wanted to go back. His aversion to Riverside Park began the evening his father interrupted an episode of *Lost in Space* to tell Mark, "I've decided to sign you up for Little League," then headed toward the kitchen to make the call.

Mark leapt to his feet. Catching his father by the arm, he implored him not to make him play.

"It will be good for you," Pierce said as if he had some secret insight into him that Mark didn't have himself. No matter how Mark begged, Pierce held to his decision. Mark's weepy pleading only made his father more determined. Exhausting his arguments, Mark finally flew to his bedroom as his father made the call to sign him up for the St. Linus Mavericks t-ball team.

Sobbing into his pillow, Mark didn't hear Nicki come in.

"What's the matter?"

"Go away."

"Don't be a baby, just tell me what's wrong."

He looked into Nicki's cat eye glasses, but the words were a tightening noose that left him struggling for breath.

"You're gonna give yourself an asthma attack. Tell me." He couldn't. His mind jumped to imagining her reaction. She always took their father's side. If Mark argued with her, she would remind him when Dad knew what was best for them before they knew themselves. He didn't want to hear it.

"Go away."

Nicki grimaced. Mark was surprised at the power of his anger. Shutting her out hurt her. He formed a gentle apology in his mind, but before the words came out, Nicki stepped toward the door with a haughty swagger. "Sissy." The word struck him with such force he felt something in him shift. His helplessness became smoldering rage. Though generally passive, Mark could be stubborn and willful. By the time he had fallen asleep, exhausted from the tears that refused to stop despite his steely will, Mark determined to make his father regret his cruel decision. I'm no ball player, thought Mark, and, by God, he's gonna know it too before the season is over.

Proving his incompetence required much less effort than Mark expected. He had no coordination either catching or throwing anything, even a large and cushioned t-ball.

Being on the field mortified him. Even his defiance couldn't diminish that. But he could withstand the humiliation knowing he would prove his father wrong. He did NOT know better than Mark what was good for him. Not this time.

During practice Mark ignored his teammate's jeers whenever he made an embarrassing error. He could tolerate a little verbal taunting if it convinced his father never to force him into doing what he hated. Throughout most of the season nothing, not even his mother's encouraging cheers from behind the backstop, curbed his vengeance.

Luckily for Mark the coaches discovered immediately that his lack of interest matched his lack of talent. It was seldom a problem leaving Mark on the bench. Mark never objected, and the team was better for it.

Mark's indifference left Coach Williams entirely cold to him, which was fine with Mark. In another context, where he felt like a human being instead of his father's cause, Mark would have sought his coach's respect. Even as young as he was, Mark was sensitive to the fact that men tended to dismiss him.

Had Assistant Coach Lockhart been like Williams, Mark could have finished the entire season without playing at all. But Lockhart took pity on Mark and invited him to warm up with the rest of the team before one mid-season game. The man's compassion moved Mark, who felt ashamed of his ineptness.

"Just do your best," Lockhart patted Mark's back reassuringly as the players took their positions around the field. Mark's heart pounded. He looked at his assistant coach, grateful for his kindness. No man had ever taken an interest in Mark. When Lockhart nodded encouragingly from the dugout, Mark's angry resolve faltered. Even if it pleased his father, Mark couldn't disappoint this kind man. As the team peppered the ball, Mark grew eager to catch rather than dodge it, as he usually did. Watching the ball sail from player to player, he anticipated the sting of its landing in his mitt. Unfortunately, to watch the ball, Mark held his mitt too low.

Lockhart's "Watch it!" came too late. The ball soared right at Mark's face. The blow knocked him backward. Blood gushed from his mouth where two front teeth had been secure seconds earlier.

In panic and curiosity the team hovered around Mark. Quickly, worried expressions gave way to laughter and imitation. Even if he weren't in pain, Mark would have been indifferent to their ridicule. He was focused exclusively on someone else.

Lockhart knelt beside him, one hand firmly cradling Mark's head, the other applying pressure to his mouth with a towel. "It's okay, buddy," he assured, trying to mask his guilt for asking Mark to do what he obviously couldn't. Mark felt awful for disappointing this man. The kinder he was, the worse Mark felt.

"I'm thorry," Mark mumbled through the blood-drenched terry cloth. By game time, Mark's mouth had stopped bleeding and Lockhart had driven him home.

It took Mark a week to find courage enough to return to practice. When he did, he felt even greater resentment toward his father and stronger resolve to make up for disappointing his kind assistant coach. An opportunity came early in the game when Lockhart's son Billy, who was too little and too young to play anyway, made the absolute unforgivable error: He struck out. In t-ball, with the ball immobile on a rubber tee in front of the batter, this was nearly impossible. The entire crowd gasped in consternation.

Courageously the young boy fought back tears as he passed his father, who could barely disguise his own disappointment. Billy sat beside Mark behind the dugout fence that separated the two of them from the rest of the team. Mark hated to see Coach Lockhart so disappointed.

Mark's mind reeled until it reached an obvious solution. That same inning Mark went up to bat. In his fiercest stance he swung mightily, flailing the bat several inches above the ball and nearly dislocating his shoulder with determination. Strike one.

Had he gotten an encouraging response from Coach Lockhart, he might have reconsidered his plan. But when all he heard from behind were grumbles from the head coach, Mark was determined to follow through. He dug one foot into the dirt and swung again, this time smacking the tee beneath the ball, causing a shallow thud as the ball flew backward toward the catcher. Strike two.

Finally Mark decided he had enough coordination to make this attempt look authentic. He cocked the brim of his cap, pulled back for a powerhouse hit, then swung the bat so close to his target that a gust of wind from his swing brushed the ball, making it drop with a tiny "dup" on the rubber base of the tee. Mark had struck out.

He feigned disappointment as he returned to the dugout bench. "See," he told Billy, "it could happen to anybody."

The little boy smiled in relief, then turned hopefully toward his dad. The pain in Coach Lockhart's face eased. He nodded reassuringly to his son.

That moment was the highlight of Mark's season. Knowing his father was there to see him strike out made it priceless. In that one action, he had not only made up for disappointing Coach Lockhart, but he also won the battle of wills against his father.

Even at season's end when the team took first place, Pierce never tried to convince Mark it was all worthwhile. He knew better. Mark had proved it once and for all: He was not going to do what he didn't want to.

Chapter

5

"We're out of cigarettes," Russell said to Mark as they pedaled down Beech Daly. "Let's pick some up at P & L." Russell turned onto Hass without waiting for Mark's reply. Though willing to split the cost of cigarettes, Mark never had the nerve to buy them. "You go. I'll wait here with the bikes," Mark offered as they stopped in front of the little market across from St. Linus.

"Don't be scared. We're going in for a purchase, not a holdup. Come on."

In the market Russell asked the snarling old woman behind the register for a pack of Kools. "I need your half, too," he told Mark while digging in his pocket.

Mark was so nervous he dropped his money on the counter. The sweaty change bounced to the floor.

"You boys are too young to smoke," she insisted, then paused to vacuum up a lung full of her own cigarette.

"It's not for us," Mark replied.

She swiped the Kools off the counter. "Get out of my store."

Mark was so stunned he couldn't lift his feet.

Unfazed, Russell stared at her for an interminable second. "If you don't want our money, we'll go somewhere else."

"It's not the money," she growled and looked at Mark, "I don't like liars."

Mark stared at the leathery old woman disdainfully. More disturbing than the hard crevices of her cheeks, the bulbous wrist bone, or even the shaky yellowed fingers were her accusatory eyes. They saw through his weak lie so easily.

When energy returned to his feet, Mark left Russell alone to haggle with old horsehide. Mark hated being so transparent.

I'm not a good liar, he thought. From now on, I'd rather keep secrets than tell lies.

"She wouldn't sell me the cigarettes," Russell reported as he mounted his bike.

"There are other stores."

"Oh, I'll get cigarettes here one day. You watch me."

They got a pack of Kools and even a free book of matches from a convenience store on Ford Road before racing to the clay mounds at the end of Kinloch Park.

Lying out of view from passersby, they watched their smoke rings disappear overhead.

"You ever smoke pot?" Russell asked once he nestled into his philosophical mood.

"No. You?"

"No." He took another drag and let it out slowly. "Ever want to?"

"You got some?"

"No. I just wondered if you ever cared to."

"No."

"Me neither. Does your sister?"

Mark used to reflexively defend Nicki, but his new decision not to lie made him consider his answer. "Maybe she's tried it. Do you think she has?"

"I don't know."

After a comfortable silence Russell began again. "I guess that kind of thing comes with high school."

High school. The words impaled Mark. "I wouldn't know," he snapped.

"Well neither would I," Russell shot back with more surprise than real anger.

Mark hated how quickly fear could slice through him. "I don't want to talk about it."

"You don't have to try anything you don't want to. Not everybody smokes pot. Just 'cause your sister's—"

"Forget my sister."

"Sorry. I don't care. She's nothing to me."

Mark's nervous heart pounded so hard he could feel the back of his eyes throbbing. "Let's go do something."

"Want to go to my house?"

Russell's suggestion surprised Mark. His place was generally off limits to children. Russell's father, though only in his late fifties, was a frail, sickly man who seldom left the house since his accident. Five years earlier he'd fallen down an elevator shaft and crushed most of the bones in his back, legs, and feet. After excruciating rounds of restorative surgery and physical therapy, he was ambulatory, though any movement seemed like a shifting, sliding struggle.

"Your house?"

"We sure can't go back to yours. Everything's torn up." Mark found Russell's dad pretty eerie, but right now being spooked seemed better than feeling so annoyed. "All right."

Heading up Russell's drive, Mark asked, "Is your dad home?"

"I think he's in the basement fixing the picture tube of our old television. He's good with stuff like that."

"What about your mom?"

"I don't see the car."

Russell led Mark to the basement. "Wait here."

From the foot of the stairs Mark watched Russell approach his father in the dimly lit corner of the room. He was a little man (he'd lost more than an inch as a result of his accident) with dark eyes that swam behind thick glasses. Russell had to speak softly into his ear for conversation, so Mark never heard what they were saying.

Watching Russell and the shadowy mass of illness that was not like his father at all, Mark studied postures. Russell looked authoritative standing beside his dad, speaking to him clearly and watching his father's expression to make certain his words were understood. Mark couldn't imagine taking such a stance with his own dad. He never felt that confident around him. It was a nice scene to observe. Mark seldom saw two guys connect like that.

"My mom went grocery shopping in Windsor," Russell offered as he led Mark back up the stairs, "so the house is ours. Let's play cards."

Mark didn't notice the time until Russell's mother returned and asked him to stay for dinner. He jumped up. "Oh man, Russell, I'm late!" He thanked her for the invitation and hurried off.

Mark raced around the court so intent on getting home he didn't see his neighbor backing out of the drive. By the time the chrome bumper caught the setting sun and blinded Mark, Mr. Nerus's station wagon was already barreling toward him. The corner of the bumper clipped Mark's back tire, slinging him high into the air toward the plush grass connecting their yards.

Amil Nerus slammed to a stop and rushed to Mark's aid. "My God, where'd you come from?"

"I didn't see you!" Mark trembled.

"It's okay, son," he lifted Mark effortlessly. "I didn't see you either." Though no taller than Mark, Amil was broad and sturdy. "Are you all right?"

Mark was captivated by the concern expressed from a masculine voice. "I'm fine," he assured before he even knew.

"You're not hurt?"

Mark slapped the grass stains on his knees. "No." He was more sure now.

Standing eye-to-eye with Amil, Mark felt like a man. "I'm okay." Then he turned to see his twisted tire rim. "My bike!"

As Amil lifted the bicycle, Mark watched the veins in his forearm branch out and disappear under a field of dark hair. He glanced at his own arm to compare them.

"It's just a bent rim. I can replace that for you."

Mark looked up expecting to see Amil's dark, round cheeks and narrow chin in profile as he inspected the bike. Instead he was shocked to see Amil's brown eyes looking directly at him. "You don't need to fix it."

"Course I do. But first we need to take care of you. You didn't hit your head, did you?"

"No," he said without thinking.

"If you did it could be dangerous."

Just then Sao Nerus bounded through the front door. The youngest of Amil's daughters, she was short and pudgy, with a broad mouth that dominated her chocolate face.

"Dad, I thought you left."

"No, I—"

Stepping forward to get his bike, Mark teetered. Amil grabbed his forearm to keep him from falling. "You all right?"

"What happened?" asked Sao.

"Nothing!" Mark shouted.

"It was my fault."

"No, I just fell."

"Gah," her jaw dropped.

"Sao, go in the house," her father said. "I'm just running an errand. I'll be back before dark."

"It's almost dark now."

"Go in the house."

"Gah," she muttered and left.

"I need to tell your parents what happened."

"No, I'm okay."

"What if you hit your head?"

"They're not home," Mark insisted, wanting this embarrassing incident behind him.

"Then I'm coming back to check on you."

"I'm fine."

"Promise me you won't go to sleep until your parents get home and you tell them what happened."

"Don't go to sleep?"

"You might never wake up."

Mark didn't understand.

"Come on, let me take you in my house. You can stay with Mrs. Nerus until your folks return. Where are they, anyway? Your mother's not usually gone."

"Don't know. But I'll be fine. I won't go to sleep."

"You promise?"

"I won't."

"I'll check on you later."

"You don't need to."

"All right." Amil nodded. "I'm gonna take you at your word."

As he watched Amil drive away, Mark was overcome by a ravenous desire to honor Amil's faith in him. For the first time, Mark felt like a man. He would keep his promise not to sleep, if not for himself, for Amil, whose secret trust he would not betray.

Mark hid his bike between the folded ping pong table and the garage wall, then braced himself as he entered the kitchen. No one was there. Mom's radio wasn't playing. The electric skillet wasn't sizzling and nothing simmered on the stove.

"Hello?" Mark proceeded to the living room. "Mom?"

When he didn't find her there, or in the bedrooms or bathroom, he returned to the kitchen table and looked for a note. There was none.

He opened the basement door. Descending the stairs, he heard running water. "Mom?"

Hunched over the cement laundry tub, she was scrubbing a sock against the washboard and crying.

"Mom, what is it?"

She looked at Mark, squinting with anger. "Did I tell you to watch him? Didn't I say, 'Keep an eye on your brother, Mark'?"

"What happened?"

"Your father took Brandon to the hospital. Just got home from a business trip and had to race to emergency."

"My God, why?"

"Brandon fell on some metal stripping and cut his leg wide open. You're just lucky your father got home right then or there's no telling what could have happened to your little brother." She turned back to her work. "And don't say, 'My God'."

"Sorry."

She swiped her forehead with the inside of her wrist. Her voice softened. "He's only a baby, Mark. He doesn't know what can happen. I was depending on you…"

"I didn't know. He was out playing with Sao when Russell and I left." Knowing he'd gone to smoke tweaked Mark's guilt.

"I can't watch him twenty-four hours and do everything else. That's why I need you, Mark."

"I know." Mark's head began to pound. "Is he going to be all right?"

"You should see the gash across his little leg. He'll need a tetanus shot and stitches." June stiffened. "It's that damn pool. He's just got to have his big, impressive toys, doesn't he?"

"Who?"

"First it was moving. We had that nice frame house on Silvery Lane, but no, he wanted brick. So we moved here. Now what? A pool. Do we know anyone with a built-in pool? Not a soul. But your father, he's gotta be the first, doesn't he? Always the first, always him. And look what happens. I'm so tired of it already."

Mark came closer and rubbed his mother's shoulder. "Brandon will be all right, won't he?" He waited for her reply. "Mom?"

She shook a thought from her mind. "Oh, sure, he'll be fine. But I bet he'll have one beaut of a scar."

"What can I do for you?"

"Do you know where your sister is?"

"I haven't seen her."

"I tell you, Mark, things are falling apart." She rinsed the sock under the tap. "Between your father and your sister, I don't know how much more I can stand."

"What do you mean?"

"Oh, you don't need to hear this. You're just a boy." She turned off the water. "Mark." His name consumed the sudden silence. "You know I depend on you?"

"I know." Mark struggled to read the thoughts behind her anguished expression.

"You're not going to let me down, are you?"

"How do you mea—? No, Mom. Course not. I won't let you down."

"People are always letting each other down. But you boys, you and Brandon, I have hope for you two. I mean, I don't know about Brandon, he's just a baby. But with you, it's different. Do you know what it means, Mark, to trust somebody like I trust you?"

He wasn't sure what she meant, but he felt the burden of it. "Yes, Mom, of course I do."

"I know you didn't mean to let me down. I think everything'll be okay. Your dad and Brandon will be home soon. We'll all be here, just like when you kids were little. I like that."

"Yes."

"We won't eat till late now, but it won't be the first time, will it?" her voice filled with hope.

"No."

"You'll start getting things ready for us? Set the table and make a salad? Your sister should be home soon from God-knows-wherever she is and she'll make us some pork chops. Your dad likes pork chops. It'll be a good homecoming meal, don't you think? I'll help you when I'm done down here." Picking up Brandon's other sock, she returned to her task with the same intensity as before. Mark watched her, the grating of knuckles against tin sparking a sudden headache.

She wrapped the sock around her fingers to inspect the threads. "My God, he got blood all over everything."

At 8:00, Pierce and Brandon returned from the hospital. With Nicki frying pork chops and Mark setting the table, June hurried into the kitchen to check on Brandon. "How's my little man?"

"Fine. I have five stitches," he bragged. "Five."

June lifted his leg and kissed around them before Pierce set Brandon down. "You're a brave boy."

"I cried," he admitted, "but they gave me candy so I'd be quiet."

Pierce smiled through his fatigue. "He had the whole emergency room distracted."

"I got louder so they'd give me more."

"Brandon!" Mark scolded.

"It didn't work, so shut up."

"I bet you're hungry." June's sweet tone soothed the tension.

"I want apple sauce."

"We've got apple sauce for you, baby. And pork chops, mashed potatoes, corn."

"I made a salad."

"I want apple sauce."

"You'll get your apple sauce," June assured as they all took their places around the table.

Pierce laced his fingers and led the grace. "Bless us, oh Lord…"

Glancing at his father's praying hands, Mark noted unmistakable white arcs where he should have clipped his fingernails. In contrast, Mark's nails were neatly trimmed. His look like a girl's, Mark thought, and felt proud for being more masculine than his own father.

"How was your trip?" June always asked the question without any spark.

"You know, things are coming along really well."

"Mark, pass your father the potatoes." She looked across the table. "Coming along well, huh?"

"Things are going to be so great once the modules are completed."

"Did you want more oleo on those potatoes?"

"No. Once they're completed, we ship them from Oshkosh to the Holiday Inn site in Pontiac, and the project is underway. This is big, June, really, really big."

"Yeah, you've said. By the way, our electric bill is due." The tea kettle whistled, drowning out Pierce's assurance that he had the money to cover it.

June poured the hot water into her cup. The crusty, used tea bag softened and drooped in the liquid heat.

"Ow!" Brandon jolted.

"What is it, son?"

"Mark just hit my leg with the stitches."

Mark nearly dropped his fork. He'd been eating quietly this entire time and never moved enough to touch Brandon, even accidentally.

Brandon swung his leg from under the tablecloth so everyone had a good view of the stitches.

Nicki frowned. "Do you mind? We're trying to eat here."

"Nicki!" scolded June. "It's all right, Brandon. I'm sure

Mark didn't mean to touch it."

"I didn't do anything!"

Pierce squeezed Mark's shoulder. "Just be careful."

"Be careful? I didn't—"

"Okay," Nicki snapped. "We know you're perfect. You didn't do anything."

Everyone watched Mark for a response. His ears reddened with anger, but he remained composed. "I didn't," he said, then stared at his plate while he finished his meal.

"Let me see that leg," June offered in her most patient voice. Brandon had to push back his chair a bit to swing his right leg toward her.

From the corner of his eye, Mark watched his mother gently scratch around Brandon's stitches. He felt lonely.

Nicki pounded her knuckles on the table. "If you're gonna do that," she told her mother, "would you at least do it under the table so the rest of us can eat?"

June flipped the corner of the tablecloth over Brandon's leg, then looked up resentfully. "Do you hear the way she talks to me?" June asked Pierce.

"Nicki—"

"Oh, I know," she cut him off, then resumed eating.

"Apologize to your—"

"I will!" Then she mumbled, "Sorry."

Brandon squirmed then leaned toward June.

"What is it?"

He nuzzled against her arm and her expression softened. Mark watched Brandon's eyes roaming possessively toward Nicki.

She stopped chewing. "My new friend came by the

bank again today," she began.

Mark turned to catch Pierce's expression. They all knew why she began any dinnertime story.

"Friend?" June asked, and Pierce rolled his eyes. "I don't remember a new friend."

"I've mentioned him before."

"Him?"

"Yes, him. Women can have male friends, Mom."

Mark watched the vein in his dad's neck throb. "Who is this friend?" Pierce asked. "Do we know him?"

"No."

"Is he in any of your classes?" he asked.

"I met him at the bank, not at school. I just told you that."

"He doesn't go to Divine Child?"

"He's college age."

Pierce's anger swept a wave of heat across the table.

"What college does he go to?" June asked with exaggerated civility.

"I didn't say he goes to college." Nicki paused for effect. "I said he was college age." She took a bite to leave a silence before her next comment. "He quit school when he was fifteen."

The crevices around Pierce's mouth reddened. He stifled his next comment with a mouthful of pork.

"He's doing really well now, earning good money. Kinda makes you think, doesn't it?"

Mark couldn't help himself. "What about?"

"You know, choices." She looked toward her father. "Things we think we have to do to be happy and successful."

"Look. I'm tired. It's already been a bad homecoming with your brother hurt and all. Lay off me tonight."

While the red flags went up for Mark, June, and even Brandon, sometimes Nicki just couldn't resist pushing things too far. "I don't know what you mean. I was only making a simple commen—."

Everyone froze as Pierce inhaled his anger so deeply his nostrils whistled louder than the tea kettle. He stood and hurled his fork across the room. It hit the tile behind the stove then bounced on the turquoise carpeting. "Just five minutes home. Five damn minutes." He grabbed his keys from the junk table and left the house.

Mom glared at Nicki. "Sometimes…"

Nicki sprang up. "Everybody's so damn touchy in this house. And always when he comes home." She stormed down the hall and slammed her bedroom door.

Chapter

6

Holed up in her room before going out, Nicki vented to her only confidante.

> *Oh Leda,*
>
> *I don't know why he gets to me like that. What happens to me when I'm around him? I can be such a bitch.*
>
> *You think I'm crazy? I don't either really. But I can't explain it. It's like a snake rattling inside my stomach then jumpin' outa me and striking at him. As much as I hate myself afterwards, I gotta admit I like the charge I get out of him. Getting to him makes me feel powerful.*
>
> *Okay, onto better topics. Tomorrow after work I'm going to see the Pink Floyd movie with Nelson and Candy. Tonight I'm off to see Toke.*
>
> *Hey, BIG EVENT: I'm in business now. Toke's been having a little financial trouble jump-*

starting his jewelry sales, so he asked me to pitch in a couple hundred dollars in exchange for a percentage of his profits. Is that cool or what? I'm an entra--, entripren — I'm the Gloria Steinem of costume jewelry.

BIG EVENT 2: the top layer of the back yard is gone and the pool area has been marked off. It's bigger than I thought it'd be. Bigger, I bet, than any of us expected. Cool. Time to get ready. Party.

N

As in the past, loneliness approached June stealthily, caught her off guard so she couldn't defend herself against it. By the time she recognized its return, it had already devoured her like the tide coming in at night—black, quiet, and endless.

Sitting alone on her bed, she felt an overwhelming need to be comforted. An old, once familiar intonation seeped through her mind. Comfy, honey? This time, even drawing forth that memory didn't help.

Because her loneliness confused her, she judged it as selfish and unacceptable. She'd never seen it in her own mother, who masked her fears with humor. There were no signs of these questionable stirrings in either of her beloved aunts. Honey had magnetic friendliness and no-nonsense courage that came from running her corner bar. Stas, who, after the sudden death of her husband and a subsequent miscarriage during the War, conquered grief by facing the rest of her life with fearless enthusiasm.

June was like none of them: not funny, gregarious, or resilient. She couldn't imagine other women feeling the emptiness that now overwhelmed her.

She couldn't stand it. This time she had to reach out to someone. Father Slaughter. She could talk to her priest about her "loss."

That's what I'll call it, June thought. It was an apt description. This feeling felt like mourning. She put on a better outfit and applied some makeup, mostly to cover the dark circles from her afternoon of tears.

In the kitchen, she scribbled a note to Nicki not to leave until she returned, then headed toward the door. From the living room, Mark called for her.

"I'll be back in a minute," she said without stopping.

On the way to the rectory, she practiced what she would say. Expressing her feelings aloud made them sound so selfish. She was married to a good, hard working man. She had three healthy children. They never went hungry, they had a nice house. For God's sake, she was about to own the only built-in pool in town. What did she have to complain about?

With doubts enveloping her, June pulled up to the rectory but sat in her car, engine running, lights off. She stared at the porch trying to muster enough courage to approach it. She sat there so long her loneliness turned to anxiety. She couldn't do it. She flicked on her headlights and returned home.

Mark lay on the living room couch, his head throbbing.

"Don't go to sleep," Amil had told him. "Promise you won't go to sleep before telling your parents what happened." Now they weren't even home.

The pressure in Mark's head matched the tension still lingering in the house. Every room felt like an over-inflated tire. He hated it.

"Don't go…to sleep," an inner voice said to the rhythm of his throbbing temples. "Don't go…to sleep."

Mark stepped outside for some air. Beyond their suffocating house, everything looked so expansive, it took his breath away. The sky, speckled swaths of azure and ebony, continued forever. Behind his house, a distant light shone over the trees. His heart leapt.

How did I forget? He climbed onto the backyard barbecue grill, grabbed the gutter of the house, and lunged onto the roof.

From a mile away, the Dearborn Drive-In theater screen appeared above the trees. His dad introduced Mark to this discovery when he was only four. The thrill remained so vivid that Mark's throat tickled whenever he returned to this spot. It was the best moment he and his father ever had together.

The Poseidon Adventure was appearing for its last few days at the drive-in. Some nights, Mark sat and watched the entire film even though he was much too far from the theater to hear anything. Tonight, he lay back to watch just as the capsized ship was rocked by its first explosion.

Before the scene ended, he heard his mother drive up. He didn't call out to her, but remained still until she went into the house. Then he continued watching the movie.

As the ship's passengers struggled through one obstacle after another, Mark noted how they worked together to help each other climb. In the end, the least exceptional people would survive. Both ideas filled Mark with hope.

Just before Gene Hackman leapt onto the red valve, Pierce returned home. Keeping perfectly still, Mark lay flat against the roof, listening for footsteps to disappear into the house as his mother's had an hour earlier. Instead they approached the backyard and faded as his father trod through the piles of dirt making way for a new pool.

Mark watched his father from above. Pierce traversed each mound, sure-footed even in the darkness. Where the lawn now ended and the black earth dipped, Pierce stopped. Motionless except for his breathing, he stared at the concave mass for what seemed an interminable time.

As far away as he was, Mark sensed a tension in his father's countenance. From his proximity Mark couldn't tell if it was excitement or anxiety. His father turned around just once to look back at the house. He shook his head and ran his forefinger down the corner of his mouth.

Turning back to the exposed earth, Pierce inhaled so deeply Mark thought he heard his dad's nostrils whistle as they had at dinner. Finally Pierce bent down and picked up a handful of clay, and kneaded it until it fell, bit by bit, through his fingers. When the pieces were gone, he brushed the dirt from his palm, and went into the house.

Mark waited until he heard the front door close before sitting up again. He looked at that big, shapeless plot and wondered what his father could have been thinking as he stared at it so long. Just then, the sky brightened. Mark looked past the trees. It was the light of rescue for the six remaining passengers at the end of the movie. After their night in the mangled rubble of the S. S. Poseidon, a rescuer's torch cut open the hull and morning flooded in. The screen lit the sky.

In the still summer night, Mark crept down from the roof and crawled through the window onto his trundle bed. Leaning back on his pillow, he realized his headache was gone.

Nicki arrived at his apartment so late, Toke was already getting ready for bed.

"Hey," he let her in. "I didn't think you were coming. Make yourself comfortable. I'm about to get a quick shower."

While waiting, Nicki wrote him out another check as promised and left it on the counter. She grabbed a green apple from his refrigerator, but it was so bitter, she threw it away.

Bored, Nicki gazed around his sparse apartment and decided he must be lonely. He seldom mentioned other people. His family lived out-of-state. Besides her, he didn't seem to have anyone.

When she got tired of waiting, Nicki resumed work on some of the wood nail rings they'd begun the other night. The materials they'd been using were still set out, but Nicki wanted to try the new florescent paints she brought the previous week. After looking everywhere else, she went into the bedroom and started searching through Toke's dresser. From the bottom drawer, a pungent sting of bad perfume surprised her. So did the unexpected array she discovered. Inside were women's toiletries, a few changes of clothes, and some scant undergarments. Buried beneath it all was a stack of pictures. Nicki flipped through them. They were nothing lewd, just friendly snapshots from a camping trip and a few at someone's kitchen table. Each photo included one or two women, perhaps sisters or friends.

Apparently it was the thin brunette Toke liked. She was in every picture. The other woman, who had a heart tattoo on her thigh and was too fat for the clothes she wore, appeared off to the side in only a few exposures.

Toward the bottom of the stack, Nicki found two snapshots of the brunette leaning over a bathtub with a little kid in a cloud of soapsuds. Nicki looked close to see if the child resembled Toke, but the photos were too blurry.

When the shower cut off, Nicki replaced the pictures, closed the drawer, and was back in the living room before Toke returned. They worked on rings late into the night, but she never questioned him about the brunette. At first she didn't know how she felt, but as she drove home, Nicki was relieved that he had a woman and even that he kept secrets. It assured her that Toke was okay with their platonic friendship, and it gave her the freedom to harbor secrets of her own.

Nicki knew she shouldn't have violated her curfew again, but she figured, What the hell? he's already mad at me. He won't do anything about it anyway.

She pulled into the drive. As always, the house was dark except for two rectangular beams shooting out the vertical windows of the front door. He was waiting in the hall again.

She flung her purse over her arm and barreled into the house.

Nicki learned to gauge her father's anger by his robe belt. If it was pretty loose, she'd get by with a mere scolding. Taut little creases in the waistline meant trouble.

Tonight, the belt was so tight she could make out the curve under his ribcage. Waiting for him to speak, she listened to the drone of his nostrils.

He shook his head and stroked the protruding slash of crimson that cut his mouth into a frown. "Well?"

What could she say? As always, she wasn't doing anything bad. But she'd told the truth before and he never believed her. She shrugged in reply.

"I'm taking away your car."

Nicki froze, determined not to let him see her shock. Think, think. She took a breath so she wouldn't seem riled. "You can't do that. It's my car."

"I co-signed for it."

"But we agreed. I make the payments myself. I never ask for help. It's mine."

"You've abused your privilege. You know when you're supposed to be home. I can't wait up for you all the time like this. Now I won't have to."

"Okay, you won't have to. I won't be late again."

"You're right because I'm taking your car."

"But, Dad."

"Give me the keys."

"You don't mean it. You're just mad. Let me explain."

"Don't argue with me. I'm too tired. I've waited up till 1:30 worrying about somebody who obviously doesn't give a damn. I'm not up for a discussion. Give me the keys."

Shaking venomously, Nicki could not make herself hand them over. "I wasn't getting into any trouble. I was at a friend's place. I didn't call—"

"—because you didn't want to wake everybody up. I know, Nicki. I've heard it before."

"It's the truth."

His sour look told her what he suspected. "I wasn't doing anything bad."

"I didn't say you were. What made you think I was accusing you? Guilt?"

You son-of-a-bitch, she thought. You don't even know the first thing that's going on with me. "You want my keys? Here." She thrust them forward.

He pried them from her defiant fingers.

"Is that it?"

"Don't you smart off to me."

One breath. Two. Then calmer. "Is that all?"

"That's all. Good night."

As her father turned to leave, words passed Nicki's tongue like dry ice. "I work Saturday morning at 7:00. You gonna be up by 6:30 to take me or should I quit?" Though burning, Nicki reveled in the heady power billowing through her. She stared him down.

Instead of answering, he scraped his mouth once more

then disappeared down the hall, traces of anger dragging behind his lumbering footsteps.

Chapter

7

The next morning, Mark's headache had not returned and everything seemed back to normal. In the kitchen his mother sat in her same vinyl chair, legs tucked beside her, head tilted forward, gaze distant and abstracted. Except for slender fingers tracing the handle of her teacup, she was motionless.

In her white blouse and black-and-white hound's tooth pedal pushers, she was a weighty stone amid the flowing air of colors around her. On the turquoise tablecloth stood a red cup, a yellow lemon-shaped squirt bottle, and a vibrant floral centerpiece. Behind her, the brown refrigerator sported an orange cookie jar in the shape of Tony the Tiger.

The morning light silhouetted her profile with perfect beauty. Even in her daily colorlessness, she was the vivid presence for Mark.

"Mark, honey, I want us to wash these windows. I know we just did them, but look," she pulled aside the shear curtain. "It seems like I'm forever re-doing what's been done and nothing stays clean. Dirt's so thick you can barely tell it's morning."

Mark ignored her exaggeration. "Sure, I'll help you," he reached for a box of Life cereal on the high shelf. "I'll go to Wise Owl early today."

"That's fine. Meanwhile I'll wash these curtains. They're as dirty as the windows."

Despite his leg wound, Brandon raced up the huge mound in the backyard and slid down its side. Then he lay very still, a soldier scanning his territory for the enemy. If June found him here, she would banish him from the back yard until construction was over.

"Morning, Brandon," Frank Willis called as he and the crew began another day's work.

Brandon waved, then ducked out of sight. Needing a better hiding place, he began digging a shallow trench in the side of the mound. A few handfuls into his excavation, Brandon scooped up something hard.

At first he thought it was only a pop top, but it turned out to be a ring. Clay filled the concave setting where a stone used to be.

"I can find that diamond!" As he continued to dig, he thought, If this is here, just think of all the neat junk that's getting digged up right now. So he abandoned his trench and started searching for treasure.

Mark's weekly visits to Wise Owl Book Shoppe at Ford and Beech Daly began one evening after he and his mother left Farmer Jack. "Can I go in there for a sec?"

"Sure. I'll load up the groceries and wait for you out here. Do you want some money for a book?"

Mark lit up. "Can I?"

She gave him two dollars. "Get a receipt and bring me my change."

"Thanks!" He dashed into the store and asked the white-haired woman behind the counter if they had *The Poseidon Adventure*.

"All our movie tie-ins are right there behind you."

At the end of the last bookshelf Mark scanned dozens of paperbacks arranged alphabetically. *Carnal Knowledge, Deliverance, The Getaway*. His eyes jumped to a lower rack, *Lady Sings the Blues*, and lower, *Paper Moon, Papillon, The Poseidon Adventure*. Mark grabbed it. The cover illustration included two faces that resembled none of the cast. But on the back was a checkerboard of the stars' photos and two scenes from the movie. Mark couldn't pay for his purchase fast enough.

As he turned to leave, his eye caught the title *The French Connection*. Below it was a photograph of Gene Hackman shooting someone on an outdoor staircase. 95¢. Mark didn't have enough change. But he wanted this book, too. In fact, he now wanted every book and magazine he could find containing pictures of *Poseidon* stars.

Rather than leaving disappointed, Mark was inspired. From then on, he returned every week. Over time, his search expanded to Hollywood fan magazines against the back wall, tabloids stacked near the entrance, and movie reference books displayed beside the register. Nearly every visit provided a new book or magazine for his collection.

With his bike still broken, Mark walked to Wise Owl this time. Under the tall elms along Beech Daly, he passed old frame houses of pastel green, pink, and fading white. Excitement mounted as he crossed busy Ford Road. By the time he entered Wise Owl, Mark was so ready to spend money he might as well have left it at the register on his way to the magazines.

Flipping through *Rona Barrett's Gossip*, Mark nearly passed a photo of an almost unrecognizable Gene Hackman. Bald, mustached, and wearing large eye glasses, Hackman was crouched in shadows beside a toilet. Tools and wires dominated the scene. "The Conversation," Mark read.

Further into the magazine, Mark found an even better photo of Hackman. Dressed in a baseball uniform for a charity tournament, he was hugging all three of his children in his outstretched arms. Mark had never seen Hackman with his family before. They all looked so happy. I wish he were my dad, Mark thought.

The massive teeth of the back-hoe devoured chunks of earth and spit them onto a new mound that soon grew bigger than Brandon's. By midmorning, back-hoe operator Carl Woods was nearing the nine-foot depth that would complete the digging when he struck something solid. A rumble rocked the back yard and spewed a geyser some twenty feet into the air.

"Oh, Jesus, we hit a water line." Woods ran for cover under an eave of the house. Within seconds, the entire crew huddled beside him. They stared, waiting for the gushing to subside.

"Boss," Woods finally said, "I didn't hit just any line, did I?"

"Christ," Willis ran toward the Humphry's garage. "Ya hit the big one."

Dripping on the front porch, Willis asked June if their phone cord extended to where he now stood.

"In the garage," she pointed. "The door leading to the kitch—." She noted his soaked clothes. "What happened?"

"If I was Jed Clampett, it woulda been oil," was all he said before calling the water company.

The burst of the geyser jolted Brandon. He peered over the mound where he'd been digging. "Goooo-lly!" Seeing the crew scurry for cover turned his initial surprise into laughter.

His round blue eyes followed the jet stream up to its peak. "Golly!" he stared, wondering how all that water could be underneath there. He had to find out.

Brandon rushed to just a few feet beyond the edge of the hole, then inched his way forward. He watched the churning water swell. Heavy mist soaked him where he stood. The noise was deafening. The blaring geyser competed with rapid-fire drops pounding onto the pool that grew and grew before Brandon's terror-stricken eyes.

"Hey kid, get the hell outa there!"

The voice slapped Brandon out of his paralysis. He turned and darted away from the yard, past the house toward safety.

Willis waited until the water company shut off the main line before calling Pierce.

"Yes, sir, it was the biggie."

"But it's stopped now? You did call the water company first, didn't you?"

"Yes, sir."

"How long did it take for them to respond?"

"Time-worth or flood-worth?"

No reply.

"Bout a couple inches maybe."

"Neighbor's yard, too?"

"Oh yeah. The one next door and the one behind. All three of ya share yourselves a little lake now."

Pierce sighed. "Do I need to come right home?"

"Oh no, sir. I got a couple of the guys headin' to get some pumps. Water company said we can drain it all onto the street. Just take a few hours."

"But it'll be done today?"

"Got to. Once we drain it, the water company'll send their men out to repair the pipe. Nobody's got any water until then." He remembered the glistening lake that spread across three lawns. "Least not in the house. Got plenty out."

"Frank, I'm not finding the humor in this as quickly as you are."

"No, sir, I suppose not. 'Cause it isn't funny. But it's done and can't be undone. Just gotta get it fixed, and that's what we're doing."

"All right. Hey! Basements aren't flooding, are they?"

"Not so far. Least yours isn't. And if yours isn't, I doubt if the others are. I think we caught it in time for that."

"That's good. Does this put us way behind?"

"I already got some extra men lined up to help us out starting Monday."

"I can't affor—"

"These are my own boys. What good are sons if they can't help their dad in a pinch?"

"Frank, you don't have to—"

"I do. And I also need to figure with you the bill from the water company. We musta just miscalculated the hole."

"You mean we need to move the pool?"

"No, not if we make the deep end like a funnel. We can work the pool right around the pipe and be just fine. You think it over. I'll be here when you get home tonight. Tell me then what you want to do."

Nicki seethed about her car so late the night before that the geyser's boom didn't even wake her. When she finally looked out her window hours later, the mocha lake was just beginning to recede. She rushed to her diary.

> *Leda,*
>   *Wait till he comes home to see this! Serves*
> *him right. Taking my car away. Like I'm gonna*
> *let him get away with that. One way or another,*
> *I'll get it back. But how?*

"Nicki," June's knocking on Nicki's door caused the beads against it to rattle.

"Yeah."

"Have you seen Brandon?"

"No."

"Come help me look. He's been gone awhile and Mark is at the book store."

"Be right there."

Nicki's ritual for putting away Leda was always the same. Palming the key, she locked her diary, tucked it inside the white vinyl cover of her First Holy Communion book, then buried it at the bottom of her nightstand drawer under a box of tampons. Her brothers would never bother it there.

At her vanity, she lifted the lid of her jewelry box. "The Dance of the Sugar Plum Fairies" tinkled as the plastic ballerina, minus an arm that had broken off years ago, twirled on her pedestal before a diamond-shaped mirror. Between the cardboard padding and satiny lining, Nicki always hid her diary key at the same depth, the same angle.

This time, the indentation was distorted. Her key had been removed and replaced the wrong way.

"Omigod! Somebody has been reading my diary." Nicki chucked it into her wastebasket.

"No, Mrs. Humphry," the crew members shook their heads. "Your son couldn't be in the water. I saw him head the other way, and we've been standing here since she blew."

"I can't find him!" she hurried off without waiting for a reply.

"We'll help you look, but he's not down there."

"Have you kids seen Brandon?" June asked the Nerus children coloring on their front porch.

"No, he hasn't bothered us all day."

"But we seen your flood. It's in our yard, too."

"I know. I'm sorry about that but I need to find my son." Before they could offer to help search, June ran toward the entrance of the court. "Brandon? Brandon, it's Mama!" She looked up and down the empty sidewalks of Beech Daly. "Where are you?"

The construction crew and Nerus children raced around the court in a crisscrossing, elliptical dance like the signaling of bees to honey. In their excitement, no one thought to pass through the center of the court where dwarf evergreen bushes shielded a boy small enough to hide amid them.

Through wax-drip evergreen leaves, Brandon could see into every house except his own. The others had large picture windows facing the street, but the Humphry's facade was mostly brick. Narrow panes in the front door and the frosted bathroom window revealed nothing. Even the glass to his and Mark's bedroom was partially blocked by a Russian olive tree. To Brandon it looked as though his house were hiding.

His protective haven suffocated him. Sweat trickled from Brandon's temples. The pungent pine became stifling. Caked in clay and dead evergreen sprigs, Brandon broke through the bushes.

As they saw Brandon emerge, the crew members and Nerus children lighted in their tracks. Except for the coughing pump and rushing water, the court was still. Brandon sprinted toward his mother, ankle deep in their back yard, and lunged into her arms.

"My baby." She stroked his face and head. "Brandon, where were you, baby?"

"I was scared."

"I know. The man told me. Oh, you! Don't go away like that again. Don't scare Mama like that."

"I was scared. Not you."

"Okay. Yes. Mama knows now. It's all right."

The Nerus children gathered in the soaked yard. Laughing in relief, they pawed at Brandon and eased his fear with familiar teasing. The crew members approached, taking in the exuberant scene.

"Christ," Willis turned to one of his men. "If this is how Pierce's kids react to water, why the hell is he putting in a pool?"

"Linda," Pierce stepped toward his secretary's desk, "Do you have those ledgers on the Holiday Inn account?"

"Yes, sir," she handed him the file. "And these bills," she added tentatively, "need to go out—"

"Got it," Pierce slipped back into his office and closed the door before she could question him further.

There was no money now, but in a few weeks he'd have a steady source of income: the pool. Until that opportunity came along, Pierce's money-generating ideas had all the momentum of rush hour traffic.

From the inception of The American Company, Pierce struggled alone to maintain operating costs. Sometimes he felt lucky to still have an office and enough furniture to give the impression of a fully functioning business.

"Pierce?" The heavy tone was uniquely Ed Manduski's.

"Come in."

Ed drug his huge, lethargic frame into the office. "I delivered those prints...for you. I guess I'm...done...for today...eh?"

"That's great, Ed. Why don't you call it a day?" It wasn't even noon.

"I guess I'll go then."

"See you tomorrow."

The Ed Manduski who worked for Pierce was all that remained of the tall, vibrant, very rich businessman whom Pierce asked back in 1971 to be an investor in The American Company. "Right now," Pierce had said, "highrises—office buildings, hotels—are constructed, then the bathrooms are installed piece-by-piece. If individual bathroom modules can be inserted in small office buildings, why not in high-rises?"

"Because once they're installed, there isn't enough space behind the water closets to hook them up."

"What if we inserted them back-to-back as one self-contained module," he pulled out a prototype of a plumbing tree, "then connected all bathroom pipes to the central drainage line?

"With this system, we could build fully equipped bathroom modules off-site while the highrise was being erected, then install them whole. We'd cut construction time and costs by 35%."

Ed inspected the tree. "You have the patent on this?"

"No, I took the idea to Earl Johnson."

"The engineer? Good guy."

"He helped me design it on the condition that he gets the patent and becomes the major investor in my new company. Are you interested?"

Immediately after Ed's gracious decline, Pierce's professional life accelerated as Ed's wheezed to a crawl.

With his family's savings, Pierce became president of The American Company by matching the contribution of nine investors. Before the modules brought in profits, Pierce was responsible for building, housing, and marketing the module prototypes, which he constructed in a small display shop right in Detroit.

Month by month, opportunities trickled in. American Oil liked the modules and let Pierce install one set into a service station in Utica. The small job posed no risk to them, and Pierce spearheaded the work so inconspicuously that the Unions, an overbearing and recession-struggling stronghold, did not even object. Pierce hired a small crew, led by Willis, to build the modules, haul them to the construction site, then load and set them in place, where a plumber and electrician hooked them up and tested them.

The Utica project succeeded so astoundingly, it was soon followed by more individual Amoco jobs in Troy, as well as similar low-volume jobs for Mobil and Shell. The modules were a hit, but on so small a scale, The American Company would never survive. Something bigger had to materialize.

In 1973, it did. A representative from the national powerhouse Morgan Company, with its nearest plant in Oshkosh, Wisconsin, saw the prototypes and agreed to finance a major project on the condition that they would buy out The American Company if the project succeeded. With much more stamina and inspiration than expertise, Pierce distributed a proforma to many major industries, finally securing a contractual commitment from Holiday Inn.

There was one major hitch. The American Company had no Union ties, and the Holiday Inn project was a Union job. How could Pierce, a Detroit-based builder, possibly convince so many recession-strangled Detroit Union representatives to let him construct the modules in Wisconsin's Union jurisdiction and bring them onto a different Union site?

Negotiating a tripartite agreement became Pierce's greatest achievement. It was unprecedented. Persuading the Unions was like moving granite pillars with a feather.

In the presence of the Detroit Building Trades Council, Pierce spent hours trying to convince the plumbing Union, carpenters' Union, electricians' Union, tile setters' Union and the Teamsters to allow his units to be brought onto a Union site. They agreed on one condition: Instead of having the module work done by his own crew or Morgan Company's plant laborers, Pierce had to bring in at least one tradesman from each Union to exclusively work on and affix their Union seal to every module, including the prototypes already completed and ready for installation. Additionally, the Oshkosh plant had to allow the respective Union Business Agent to visit the site—at any time, unannounced—to assure that the agreed precedence was followed to the letter.

Replacing the non-Union manufactured prototypes with new Union-constructed units was both cost- and time-restrictive, and Pierce had no way of continually monitoring the Oshkosh work from Detroit, but those were the terms he had to meet to secure the Holiday Inn project. So he signed.

Immediately, Pierce got production modules into assembly and onto the Holiday Inn site. The prototypes arrived in perfect condition and were installed without any difficulties. When the units worked and proved even more cost-effective for Holiday Inn than they had been for Amoco, Pierce initiated full negotiations with the hotel chain to be included in its nation-wide expansion.

Pierce's advancements were especially impressive because they occurred as Detroit's building boom fizzled. Many thriving companies, like Ed Manduski's, were eroding. Had Ed not been so trusting, he might have survived the lean period. But as he worked to keep his business afloat, his partners absconded with their company's profits and left town. Even before the nightmare of personal rejection, lawsuits, and poverty came full circle, Ed Manduski was a broken man.

When Ed asked for a gofer job at The American Company, Pierce hired him without hesitation. So Ed missed spots shaving and cut his own hair with household scissors. Pierce was proud to help a good man faded by defeat.

In contrast, Pierce's newest business partner glowed like oven coils. "Hey, buddy," Bob burst into Pierce's office. "I'm late, but I'm here."

Bob spoke with casual friendliness, as if they had remained close buddies since graduating from Henry Ford Trade School twenty-two years ago. Pierce barely remembered him when he first called.

Bob tried to open his briefcase on his lap, but his round stomach pushed it off and it landed at his feet. "Heh, heh." He picked it up and went on. "I've got everything set up from the sales end. How's the pool coming?"

"Great. The crew started the other day. Digging should be completed tomorrow."

"Terrific. I tell you, Pierce, we're really onto something here. You know old Dorothy told Auntie Em that her heart's desire wasn't any farther than her own back yard. For you, that's about as true as that can get, eh buddy?"

"That's true all right."

Bob pulled a dog-eared stack from his briefcase. "Here

are the papers for the next stage of our adventure."

"Venture?"

"Venture, adventure, it's all the same. Here," he tossed the sheets onto Pierce's desk. "I'll leave these with you, give you a day or two to make sure it's all cope-or-cetic. I'm sure it is though, at least the way I remember it all."

Pierce straightened the stack and flipped through it, too distracted by Bob to focus on reading.

"So what's the little woman say about our pool plan, eh?"

"The little woman?"

"Sure. Your wife. It's guaranteed she's gonna love the pool. I just wondered how she took to the rest of the deal?"

Pierce looked up from the papers feeling compelled to reply. "Fine," he said haltingly. "Fine," and left it at that.

Chapter

8

When Amil Nerus returned home, his children bombarded him with news of the flood.

"You should have seen the back yard," said Sao. "It was like bein' at the lake!"

Amil trudged through his yard to survey the damage. With every step, the saturated lawn sucked his shoes loose. Once he kicked them away and peeled off his socks, Amil's bare feet carried him effortlessly across the chill-soaked grass.

Next door, Mark scrubbed muck off the foundation of his house. It was a filthy job that took muscle, but working up a sweat made Mark feel like a man.

"Brandon," Mark had to remind him frequently, "you're supposed to be helping me here."

"'Kay," Brandon replied, splattering another clump of dirt on the walkway to missile sound effects.

"You're just making a bigger mess than we started with."

"Wait, here it comes again." He repeated the slow-motion ascent of a great missile and hammered it for midair disintegration. Debris bounced onto the water-logged flower beds and damp pavement.

"That's it!" Mark stood.

Brandon mocked Mark with a jeer. "I'm gonna tell. Mo-om, Mo-om. Brandon's not helping me."

"I was not," Mark lied. "I was gonna beat the crap out of you."

Brandon stared, curious but unthreatened.

"Just go play somewhere else. I've got work to do." Brandon gladly accommodated.

While Mark swirled the brush to dizzying monotony, Amil approached carrying a new bicycle tire and rim. "Mark."

"Oh!" Mark was embarrassed by his high pitched inflection. He looked up at the sturdy figure of Amil.

"How are you feeling?"

"I'm fine," he stood, wiping the dirt from his hands with exaggerated roughness.

"You're not sore?"

"Oh, no," Mark assured, "I know it was an accident."

When Amil looked at him quizzically, Mark realized he meant *Are you aching?* not *Are you mad at me?*.

Of course, what adult would ask a question like that? thought Mark. Why would Amil care what I felt? Right now he felt stupid.

"I'm sorry it happened. But," Amil lifted the rim, "we can fix your bike now."

"I'll get it."

Amil followed Mark into the garage and dislodged the

bike from behind the folded ping pong table.

"You've got this buried so far back here." As Amil lifted it, the veins in his solid forearms rose like intersecting highway overpasses. "I told you I'd be back to fix it."

Although his curt inflection stung, Mark was relieved that Amil hadn't realized why the bike was tucked out of view. He never told his parents what happened.

While Amil fixed his bike, Mark tried to make conversation. "The pool will be done soon."

"Zat right?"

"It should be nice. It's kidney shaped."

"Like a kidney bean?"

"Yeah, I think so."

"You got a better wrench? This adjustable one is stripping the threads. It just doesn't grip."

Mark checked the wrench in Amil's hand to make sure he'd search for the right tool. Unsure of the size, he brought his dad's whole set.

"This one," Amil took the right one.

"Can I help?"

"Boy is that nice to hear. You know with only daughters there's no one at home that I can watch grow up to be like me."

Mark eyed Amil more closely, looking for similarities between his neighbor and himself.

"Bet your dad is glad he's got you and Brandon."

Mark noticed that Amil's cheeks were round like his own. Though set against different shades of skin, their eyebrows were both full and dark.

"Brandon's more like my dad than I am," Mark said,

not wanting to be compared to his father.

Amil got to his feet. "There." He lifted the bike and spun the new tire. "Done."

Mark reached forward as if to pull Amil back from a premature exit. "Thank you," he said a little too sharply. He wanted his next words to sound steadier, more self-assured.

"Have you seen how much is done on the pool?"

"No. No, I haven't had time to drop by."

"It's nearly all dug." Mark melted a little at Amil's direct gaze. "I can show you."

"I was going to —. Okay, sure, Mark."

Hearing his name expressed without consternation from a male voice invigorated him. Mark felt adult and alive as he led Amil to the edge of the massive hole that would soon be a pool. Between their halting comments, the pump coughed up muddy water.

"I see what you mean by the shape."

Mark tried to imagine what another man would say in response, but "Yeah" was all that came out of his mouth.

"Kidney, you say?"

"Yeah." Mark walked to the larger side of the pool. "This is the deep end," he said before thinking how stupidly obvious that was. "Nine feet deep."

"Nine?" Amil nodded. "It's deep."

"The diving board goes at this end, too."

"Good."

While Amil observed the entire vicinity corralled by surveyor poles, Mark was touched that Amil took this time out for him. The simple kindness transformed Amil in

Mark's eyes. With his rumpled shirt and disheveled hair, he seemed as unimposing a man as Mark ever met. Mark stared, creating a mental picture to draw forth later: the shiny black stubble on his full cheeks, the dry white elbows, the curve of his calves below rolled-up pantlegs.

"Your dad's done pretty good for himself."

Mark didn't want to talk about his father. "Yeah, he works really hard."

"Oh, I meant to ask, does your dad have a can of gasoline I can use? My lawnmower ran dry and I wanted to mow my front yard before dark."

"I'll get it for you." Mark returned and handed it to him.

"Thank you, Mark."

Mark deflated as Amil walked away. But his heart leapt when Amil turned and looked back at him.

"I'm glad you and your bike are okay now," Amil smiled.

With his feet firmly planted in the soaked back yard, Mark inhaled with gratitude and watched Amil disappear around the front of his house. Without moving, Mark held the image of his kind neighbor and drew it forth repeatedly throughout the day.

Right after his meeting with Bob, Pierce came home determined to share the truth about the pool with June. First, he made sure Nicki's car was in the drive and headed straight to the back yard to check for flood damage. The smell of wet clay overpowered familiar scents like freshly mowed grass, the zinnias and roses blooming in Helen Banks's garden, and burnt marshmallow still bubbling on the Davenport's grill. Though the sun had set, Pierce could see how deep the construction crew had dug.

Not bad for a crew that never built a pool before. That was Pierce's end of the deal with Bob. Rather than contract out for a crew, Pierce hired his own workers during the lax period before the modules were shipped from Oshkosh for installation.

"Hell, yes, we'll do that, Pierce," Willis assured when approached. "The first residential pool in town? We'll be makin' history."

While making history might seem a daunting dream to other men, Pierce reveled in the challenge. He wanted greatness.

With nothing to take care of in the back yard, Pierce went inside and found June ironing in the basement.

"You're home early," she propped up the iron. "I didn't even start dinner. Why didn't you call?"

"It's okay. I came to check the back yard."

"You home for the evening?"

"Yes. I'll finish the rest of today's work in my office down here tonight."

"Well, good." June resumed pressing Pierce's shirt.

"Nicki's car's still out there. No conspiring with you to get me to change my mind?"

"She hasn't said a word."

Pierce checked the back wall. "Nothing leaking down here?"

"Don't think so."

"Sorry about the flood."

"It's not your fault."

"Well—"

She hung up Pierce's shirt.

"The kids are gonna love the pool."

June nodded skeptically.

"It'll be good for all of us."

"Yeah?"

"In many ways." Pierce took a cautious breath. "Financially, too."

"Financially?"

"Yes. You don't think I'd just put a pool in our back-yard and use up savings without a financial plan."

"How much of our savings did it take? I thought you said we had none to speak of?"

"That's the beauty of it, June. Not that we don't have any, but that I didn't have to use any of our own money to put in the pool."

"Do we have any?"

"Any what?"

"Savings."

"I'm not talking about savings. I'm talking about the pool. I'm talking about new profits."

"Profits?"

"You see, June, I…we had this great opportunity."

"What are you talking about?" She turned off the iron and yanked the plug from the wall.

Pierce followed June to the wash basin. "Well…having a pool will increase the value of our house."

"For who?"

"Buyers."

"We're not selling the house." She shook hot water out of the iron. "I'm not moving."

"No, I didn't say we were. But imagine the impression the pool will make for potential buyers of different markets."

"I don't want to sell this house…"

"That's not what I mean."

". . . Strangers traipsing through it any time of day, looking at all our personal stuff. I'm not going through that again."

"We're not selling the damn house. We're selling pools." There, he said it. "June, do you remember my old trade school buddy, Bob?"

"No."

"He called in the spring. We've gotten together several times and during one visit we got the idea for the pool project. Except for the price of paying the crew, the pool cost us nothing."

"The new driveway, the repair to the water line…"

"That was my fault. My crew had never dug a pool before. How would they know—?"

"Never—?"

"June, you know my guys never dug a pool before. But if I'd hired a pool company, we couldn't have afforded it."

"So we're getting a free pool?"

"Well, no, you've gotta understand business. People don't just give things away for no profit."

"Then who's profiting?"

"We will. In a big way, too. We're the first house in Dearborn Heights with a built-in pool. It's a display model for others to imitate."

"Other builders?"

"Yes."

"You're having somebody take pictures and show them to future clients?"

"Pictures are good, too. You love pictures."

"Too? What does that mean?"

"It means we have a chance for survival." He blanched at his admission.

"Who cares about your company right now? I'm talking about our family."

Pierce cringed in confusion. "That's what we are...I thought we were...I meant the family."

She marched back to the ironing board and folded the legs with a clatter. "You're gonna have to explain this one to me. I don't get it."

A surge of energy brought rapid explanation. "We thought it would be a better selling point to have people actually drop by the pool and see it in person."

"People? You mean clients? Builders?"

"Yes, and anybody who wants a pool in their backyard."

"Aw, for crying out loud, Pierce, you mean you're gonna let strangers trample through our back yard just to look at our pool? That's your big symbol of prestige?"

"June, you don't get it."

"Oh, but I—"

"You don't, and you don't even try."

June wanted courage to rise up in her and put words to her frustration that Pierce could understand. Instead anger made her eyes well. Refusing to cry in front of him, she ran from the house. On the front porch, she was oblivious to the unusual quiet of the evening and the rare absence of children riding and skating and racing noisily around the court. In the distance, she caught the lonely figure of Nicki, suede tasseled purse over her should, standing at the court entrance. Nicki stared down Beech Daly until Nelson and Candy whisked her away in a blue Pontiac Tempest.

Needing something to do, June decided to clean out her car. With no one around to see her, she ran her finger under the garage window sill and retrieved the extra set of keys she'd hidden there.

For many years, June didn't know how to drive, and being unable to leave never bothered her. Even after she learned and had her own car, she was content to stay home most of the time. But a few months ago, when Pierce stormed out of the house with her keys in his pocket, June was overcome by a helplessness she hadn't felt since her mother died. The next day, she duplicated her car keys at Duke's Hardware, then hid the new set in the garage where no one would find them.

After gathering cups, wrappers, and garbage from the floorboard of her Mercury, June opened the trunk. The upturned carpet revealed a gap beside the spare tire. June froze as a secret idea made her heart flutter with possibilities.

"June!"

She slammed the trunk.

Neighbor Helen Banks trotted from her garage toward the Humphry's driveway. "June, I won't keep you. I've got a million things to do, so I can't be bothered talking to you too long. But I need to ask you something."

June marveled at the prospect. No one had asked her anything in so long.

"We need a fourth to finish out the season on our Thursday night bowling league at Satellite. You interested?"

"Yeah."

"You see Barbara injured her hip and —"

"Yeah."

" — I know you always say no to everything, but our team's in a real bind. We start tonight at 8:00 and you're our last resort."

"I said yes."

"What—? Oh, you did, didn't you? Ha! Good! Plan to stay out late—maybe midnight or 1:00. We usually have a sandwich and drinks at the snack bar after the last game."

"Good."

"Ride with me this time. 7:30?"

"7:30."

Helen eyed June curiously. "You know, June, there may be hope for you yet."

As Helen walked away, June glanced at the closed trunk and felt both guilt and hope.

June had to suck up courage to ask Pierce's permission to go bowling. Trembling, she paused at the top of the stairs, then barreled down them before she changed her mind. "Helen said they need somebody to fill in on their bowling team."

"When?"

"Thursdays, for the rest of the season."

"Helen invited you? Next door Helen?"

She nodded.

"That's great. When do you start?"

"Tonight?" She watched Pierce roll his tongue along the inside of his cheek.

"I need to call Stan at 7:30," he replied. "Otherwise, I told you I was just spending the evening down here working. The kids can handle being unsupervised for a couple hours. You want me to pick up some A & W foot longs so we can eat before you go?"

"Helen said the girls usually stay and have a sandwich after they finish. I'll probably eat with them 'cause Helen's driving this time."

"In that case, Nicki and the boys and I will go and be back in time for me to make my call."

"Nicki's gone."

"Gone? I took away—"

"She didn't drive. Her friends picked her up in their car a little while ago."

He raised his hand to rub the side of his mouth, but stopped himself. "All right. What time you think you'll be home?"

She shrugged. "I'll be with Helen. Whenever she wants to be back. Probably after 1:00."

"I'll wait up for you."

"You know the boys can stay up past their school bedtime because it's summer."

"Okay."

"Don't let Brandon fall asleep in his clothes." She began to walk away. "And don't let him eat too much junk."

"Right."

"You know how his stomach gets."

"Yes."

"You don't want to be cleaning up vomit all evening while I'm gone."

"No."

"I mean, you'd have to. You couldn't just leave it till I got home to clean it."

"June."

He used that tone with the children. She hated it directed at her. "I'm only telling you because I don't want to find any hours-old surprises when I get home."

"For God's sake, June, give me some credit." Then his jaw relaxed. "I guess the Humphry men are bach-ing it tonight."

"I—," she couldn't even look at him to ask, "I'll need some money."

"Oh, sure," he pulled out his billfold and handed her a twenty. "Now you go and have fun."

"And you're all right with this?" He had already said so. Asking again made her feel like a child.

"Yes."

June hesitated just long enough to feel more embarrassed, then turned and walked away.

I'll never do that to myself again, she promised. Never.

Chapter

9

With Mom gone and Dad downstairs working, Mark took his newly repaired bike out for a spin. Near the entrance to the court, he joined Brandon and several other guys closer to his age in a conversation with a cluster of neighborhood men.

As Mark approached, Mr. Frederick was asking the other men if they thought he could still run a seven minute mile. He entertained comments by the guys and even by boys Mark's age.

"Maybe if you trained a little first."

"I could do that."

"You're over 30? I don't know."

"But I'm not much over, and I've stayed in shape."

"Where would you be running? Sidewalks? A track?"

"The Crestwood High track."

"Then maybe. It makes a difference."

"I think you can do it," Mark offered.

No one seemed to hear him. They continued.

"Are you psyched for it?"

"I figure if I sing in my head or think about anything besides trying hard to run it, I could make it even under seven minutes."

"Yeah, you can do it," Mark repeated a little more assertively. "There's no rea—"

"I'd pick a song with a good steady rhythm, maybe a Motown hit."

"A little Temptations?"

"No, the Four Tops."

"Or, or the Stylistics."

"Pick a Marvin Gaye tune and you'll have it. Marvin'll get you there."

As guys young and old spouted song titles and broke out in competing soulful choruses, Mark pulled away without anyone noticing. Riding around the block alone, Mark knew the truth. Among men he was no one.

What's so wrong with me? Mark wondered. Maybe I don't have much confidence, but I'm smart, I'm sensitive, creative. I like to laugh. Mom thinks I'm funny. I'm a sweet guy. I care about people's feelings. Oh God! Mark thought. I sound like a girl.

Back on the court later, Mark passed the cluster of men and boys. Instead of racing home in shame, he saw Amil Nerus and sped right up Amil's drive to thank him again for fixing his bike.

"You're welcome, Mark."

The simple interaction filled Mark with hope. Maybe I am changing, he thought after he told Amil "Good night" and went home. I'm not a cooperative Mama's Boy any more. I used to only want to please her. Now being her little helper embarrasses me. That's a good sign.

I'm not "Ma Comfy," Mark remembered the pronunciation he'd given his name as a baby that his mother loved. I'm Mark Humphry.

He liked his name. Mark. He liked the sound of it, especially from the masculine voice of Amil Nerus.

Pierce's call to contract lawyer Stan Morris that night provided better news than even he had anticipated.

"You got Hilton," was all Stan said, and Pierce's adrenaline surged.

"Confirmed?"

"Holiday Inn committed to 76 modules. Hilton is thinking 308 units for their next hotel. They're willing to sign if you're ready. Can you handle that big a job immediately?"

Stan's news accelerated Pierce toward his dream. He was so close to becoming one of the most successful men in the building industry, Pierce wouldn't let a mere time obstacle intimidate him. "Absolutely!"

When he hung up the phone Pierce shook his fists exultantly. He hungered to tell someone his good news. June was gone, but that was just as well. She wouldn't meet his exhilaration. She would cast doubts or fail to understand.

The boys wouldn't have an inkling of what this meant to him, and Nicki was gone again. Pierce thought of only one person outside of work with whom he could share his news: his mother.

Betta lived only a mile away in a little brick house down Hass Road. In 1967, Detroit race riots erupted blocks from her east side home. She was so terrified, she moved to Dearborn Heights the week of her retirement. Over breakfast every Tuesday morning, they talked politics and debated about the persecution Nixon was suffering.

Pierce dialed her number. "Mom."

"William."

The delight in her voice was all the invitation Pierce needed. He sat back in his rickety swivel chair, and excited words spilled from him effortlessly.

Whenever Nelson rounded a curve of Hines Drive too fast, Candy pressed Nicki against the passenger door. Nicki barely noticed. Except for her ego, everything about Candy was small—her body, her voice, her opinion of everyone. Nicki liked her nerve.

Candy thought she was smarter than most people. Nelson actually was. But his horn-rimmed persona was the target of such ridicule in grade school, he sacrificed intelligence for popularity at Divine Child. Though his features still didn't turn heads, his body now fit a jersey better than a lab coat.

Until recently, Nicki never paid much attention. Now she wished he, not Candy, was pressing against her.

Like Nelson, Nicki began her transformation before leaving St. Linus. She replaced her cat eye glasses with contact lenses, left early for school to thicken her make up, and hemmed her uniform so it inched up her muscular thighs.

When cosmetic changes failed to impress St. Linus classmates, Nicki altered her tastes as well. But replacing The Cowsills and Carpenters with Rod Stewart, Jethro Tull, and Stevie Wonder wasn't enough. Until "You Haven't Done Nothin'" quit feeling like a direct indictment, her metamorphosis was incomplete.

Nicki's eighth grade studies officially ended the day her letter of acceptance arrived from Divine Child. Throughout August she put on hot pants and a halter top and rode her bike to the D.C. practice field to watch the varsity football team. In response to boys' whistling, she perfected facial responses that said either "Go to hell" or "If you like me, talk to me, asshole." In her head, the relaxed harmonies of "Close to You" eventually tightened into chords of "Every Picture Tells a Story."

"Hey, put in Rod." As Nelson changed 8-traks, Nicki dropped her head back and watched the trees of Hines Drive blur from a still pleasant mix of beer and the speeding car.

When she started at Divine Child, subtle non-conformity drew no attention, so Nicki became brazen. For her first art assignment, she polished her nails in class and showed them to the teacher for a grade.

The overwhelming response it drew from classmates left Nicki speechless. Somehow they misread her fearful silence as indifference and immediately labeled Nicki "cool." She had found her new persona. So long as she remained aloof, students gravitated to her as if exploring a teasing mystery.

"Whatcha thinkin'?" Candy asked.

She shot a quick glance at Nelson. "Oh, nothing."

Over time, Nicki's popularity grew with her reputation. She did what she wanted despite, and to spite, any adult. Yet her strongest trait was her unpredictability. She partied all the time, but never got wasted. Unlike many of their friends, she avoided drugs altogether.

Nelson tilted back another swig of gin and let out a stuttering belch so loud it echoed.

"Guys are such pigs!" Candy waved the stinky air back toward Nelson.

"What do you care? It's not like I'm gonna kiss you."

Nelson leaned over. As Candy ducked, he tapped Nicki's bare thigh. "Don't get excited. I was just offering Nicki a cigarette."

"No thanks."

Nicki dressed as if she had an unslakable sexual thirst, yet responded with complete indifference to propositions and innuendoes. To her friends, Nicki was irreproachably cool.

For three years Nicki capitalized on this image. She and Candy and Nelson remained friends because of their mutual indifference to the world. But now her unexpected crush on Nelson threatened everything Nicki pretended to be. How could she confess her feelings without shattering the persona that drew his friendship in the first place?

Crammed together in the front seat of Nelson's swerving Tempest, Nicki and Candy sipped G.I.Q. Balancing a bottle of gin between his legs, Nelson steered with his knee as he lit another Marlboro.

"Nelson!" Nicki screamed as he ran off the road. He dropped the flaming match to regain control of the wheel. It was too late. At that speed, the tires couldn't grip the gravel shoulder. As the car careened across the grass and slammed into a towering maple, Nelson's gin-soaked shirt tail ignited.

For June, Satellite Bowl was a new world. The hollow smash of pins sounded nothing like whining children, and smokers' phlegm-choked laughter was nothing like the drone of clients' dull construction stories.

"You know what?" Doris inhaled a Kool, "Don's been laid off for two months, not one." With her sultry voice and black roots that unapologetically peered beneath bleached strands, Doris had a powerhouse presence.

"What do you mean?" Evelyn frowned.

Doris gripped June's arm. "Talk slow around Evelyn or you'll end up repeating yourself a lot."

June smiled.

"Evelyn, he lied about going to work for an entire month instead of admitting he lost his job."

"That's not possible. I saw him dressed and carrying his lunch pail that night we were at your place playing Bunkle."

"Bunco, Evelyn, we play Bunco," Helen rubbed her palm on a towel hanging from her huge elastic waistband.

Doris included June again. "Some of us formed a Bunco club in my neighborhood and we play once a month.

You know how?"

"With the dice?"

"Yeah."

"Yeah." June expected an invitation, but it never came.

"Anyhow, I was spending money as usual that whole month he was out of work. How was I to know? The son-of-a-bitch. He's still not working and I don't know where we're gonna find the money for this month's bills."

Helen found the game more interesting than Doris's story. "Evelyn, 't's your turn."

"Oh."

With little to offer in conversation, June spent most of the evening observing the other women.

Between turns, where she pitched the ball instead of rolled it, Doris made love to her cigarette. Her eyes closed when she inhaled. She held the smoke in until June got out of breath watching her. Then she jutted her jaw so the smoke shot exactly where she wanted it. After every puff, she slugged down rum and Cokes.

"I'm gonna get another," she waved her empty cup in front of June. "Get you something?"

"No, I don't...yeah, I'll have one, too." She reached for her purse.

"Don't insult me."

"Bu—." When Doris was far enough away, June defended herself to the others. "She said her husband wasn't working..."

Evelyn waved her bony fingers over the fan. "It won't take you long to get used to Doris . . . one way or another."

"Oh, Evelyn, shut up and bowl," Helen sighed.

Evelyn patted June's shoulder. "Poor thing, you have to live next door to her."

Being with these women made June feel alive. The emptiness that sometimes consumed her already seemed almost a memory.

Immediately after impact, Nicki flung open the passenger door and pulled Candy from the car with her. Seeing flames at Nelson's lap, Nicki thought fast and smothered the fire with a blanket from the back seat. Nelson writhed frantically.

"Don't move," Nicki hovered over him. "It's okay," she insisted until his cries subsided. "I'm here. I'm here."

Candy poked her head in. "Oh, God!"

"He's fine," assured Nicki. "Get somebody to call an ambulance."

Candy ran to a cluster of gathering people.

Nelson grimaced.

"It's just a precaution," she checked the charred shirt tail. The burn didn't seem to reach his skin. "You're all right."

By the time sirens approached, Candy had regained her composure. "I'll meet you at the hospital after I file the accident report," she told Nicki. "If he's all right, this never happened."

Nicki didn't feel scared until she sat alone in the hospital waiting room after the crisis passed. What am I gonna tell Dad? He's always believed the worst about me. This will make him think he was right all along. Damn! All those years of being basically decent shot with one stupid accident.

Then it occurred to her they probably broke some laws. Oh, God, maybe I'm in bigger trouble than I thought! She began pacing. I can't think about that now. Heart racing, Nicki stepped to the nurse's station. "I need to find out the condition of my friend, Jim Nelson."

Without looking up, the receptionist replied, "When we find out anything, we'll let you know."

Annoyed but undaunted, Nicki pressed until someone finally gave her an answer. "He's fine. Some second degree burns, but no injuries from the accident. They're dressing the wound now and he'll be released later. Are you family?"

Nicki shook her head and walked away.

Candy arrived a few minutes later with her police lieutenant father. "It's all taken care of," he assured. "You kids are damn lucky."

"Thank you, sir," said Nicki.

"Thank you, nothing. I'm not doin' this again. If any of you so much as look at another drink before you're 21, I'll arrest you myself."

After Nelson was released and he left with his parents, the lieutenant and Candy drove Nicki home.

"You need me to come in and explain anything for you?"

"What time is it?"

"Nearly 1:00."

"No, sir. My parents will be sleeping. But thank you." Nicki hurried out of the car and waved good-bye so they'd pull away immediately.

Ugh! I don't want to have to explain anything tonight, Nicki whimpered. Reaching for the front door, she heard it lock.

Oh, no!

The hall lights went off.

Nicki pressed her cheek against the door. "Dad. It's Nicki." Although the wreck gave her a legitimate excuse for being late, she couldn't tell him about that. She knocked lightly. "It's just me. I'm home."

In the silence she waited, and waited.

What do I do now?

The tumblers clicked. She took a deep breath then entered the house primed for confrontation.

"Next time," came the voice in the dark, "I don't unlock."

Closing the door behind her, she thought she heard footsteps. She turned and squinted into the black hallway. Her eyes focused on nothing. No one was there.

Down the hall, she heard her parents' bedroom door close. She stayed put, wondering what would happen next. Nothing did. She felt her way to her bedroom, then undressed in the dark and crawled into bed wearing only her bra and panties. She clutched her pillow and fell asleep thinking about Nelson.

Chapter

10

Five weeks after beginning their landmark project, Pierce's crew completed the first built-in pool in Dearborn Heights. As the last truck rumbled off the court, the Nerus girls shot like fireworks into the newly fenced-in pool area.

"When do we get to swim?" little Sao asked Brandon and Mark. Seeing the empty hole doused the girls' excitement.

"Sao!" Her oldest sister Kim slapped her shoulder. "How rude. The water's not even in yet." She looked at Mark. "When you puttin' the water in?"

"The paint on the bottom has to dry first."

"Okay," she shrugged and led her sisters home.

Gradually water from jet streams and garden hoses covered the gray painted base, crept up the fiberglass walls, and over the first blue step, then the second, then the third.

The day the pool finally filled, Pierce stayed home from work. Late that morning, he checked the water's pH then invited the family to their first swim. Nicki, Mark, and Brandon hurried to the back yard in their bathing suits.

June followed, wearing a sun dress and carrying her camera. Instead of swimming, she captured on film the rest of them enjoying the pool.

Nicki stirred the water with her foot. "It's cold," she complained, but dove right in anyway.

"I got you in action," June smiled.

Gradually, Mark worked his way down the steps, across the shallow end and into the deep. There he stood on the safety ledge until his body acclimated to the cold.

Strapped into an orange life jacket, Brandon shouted, "Take a picture of me, Mom," and jumped in without even testing the water.

"Did you get it?" He shivered, "Did you?"

June was tickled by his excitement. "Yes, Brandon."

"Did you put film in? It needed film."

Stunned, June looked at Mark, then Brandon.

"I can get you more—" Brandon saw her expression and realized what he'd just admitted. He dunked his face in the water and stayed there as long as he could.

When he ran out of breath, he bobbed up, his back to June. "Come on, Dad, let's play a game. Let's play commando like at Holiday Inn."

June was so relieved that Mark hadn't destroyed her film, she decided to postpone Brandon's punishment for another time. Watching her family all together in the pool, she snapped more pictures to commemorate the day.

"June, come in with us."

"I think I'll fix an early dinner," June replied. "You'll be hungry after swimming."

Their agreeing was just the reinforcement she wanted.

"I'll call you in when it's time to eat."

In her sentimental mood, June chose to make her Jaja's recipe for golompki. Preparing the cabbage rolls took her back to the family home in Hamtramck where she and her cousin Stephan were born, and where all the extended family lived in shifts that coincided with their factory hours.

As she cooked, June became so immersed in memories of her grandfather that she decided to bake spiced apples for dessert. Every night of Jaja's life, he placed a fresh Red Delicious on his dresser. The aroma permeated his clothes, his hair, his skin, and became the scent of all good memories from June's childhood.

With his playful gray eyes upon her, June used to struggle to absorb the Polish words that raced out of his mouth, and correct the English ones that trudged out laboriously. At bedtime every night, with an apple in one hand and Jaja's fingers gripping the other, June helped him up the stairs.

"One," she would count as they ascended the first step.

"Jeden," Jaja responded. "One."

"Good," she plodded further, "Two."

"Dwa. Two."

"Uh-hu. Three."

"Trzy. Three."

"Four."

"Jeden?"

"What?"

"One?"

"No, Jaja!" June would giggle. "Four."

"Cztery?"

"Yes. Four."

He smiled. "Oh, Cztery. Four."

Sometimes June was so overcome with love for her Jaja, she couldn't let go of his hand at the top of the stairs.

With the golompki in the oven, June gathered apples from the refrigerator crisper.

"One," she set the first one on the counter, then echoed, "Jeden."

"Dwa," came the second, keeping her in a time before so much had happened: before Ciocia Stas stood crying at the door twice, first saying good-bye to her soldier husband, later accepting condolences from a sober young officer who delivered her fate in an envelope with a Department of Army seal.

—Ring—

Before her cousin Stephan lost all hope and his pitching arm...

—Ring—

... and they hadn't yet gotten the call that Jaja...

—Ring—

... and years later the same haunting call about her own mother...

—Ring—

"Oh!" It was the phone ringing now. "Hello."

"I need to speak to Pierce Humphry, now."

"I beg your pardon," June reprimanded him like one of her own children.

"This is Hugh Sloan. Is Pierce there?"

Who do you think you're talking to? June wondered. "My husband's not available at the moment."

"When he gets there, have him call me pronto."

"Who did you say you are?"

"Hugh Sloan, the BA from Detroit local."

Detroit Local? June thought. We've only had the pool one day and already newspapers are calling. She scribbled his name on a pad. "I'll tell him." She hung up. "Eventually." Then she placed the spiced apple dish in the oven before calling the family to dinner.

As she stood at the table serving golompki, June relished having a family day like this.

"Gimme a little more," demanded Nicki.

June leered at her.

"Please."

Today especially, June didn't want confrontations over dinner. But she would not be demeaned. "You know, Nicki, sometimes intensity is not as powerful as simple kindness."

"I said please."

"And so you can have more," June slid a spoonful onto Nicki's plate.

"Thanks."

"We should have a family portrait taken sometime," suggested June. "Out at the pool."

"I like it," Pierce said, sounding more like a boss than a husband. "We ought to have a pool party, too."

Nicki's eyebrows rose. "I want a pool party. I've got lots of friends."

"I meant adults," said Pierce.

June feared he was thinking of his business associates. "Let's invite the family. I haven't seen some of my relatives since Christmas. That's just too long."

"I was thinking...maybe..."

"Or how about the neighbors?"

"The Neruses?!" Brandon asked.

Nicki tried again. "I could have some friends from D.C. over. Not too many, maybe—"

"No neighbor kids," June told Pierce as they stared each other down. "Just the adults. A cocktail party. No, a luau. That'd be perfect out there. A luau for neighbors only."

Mark's eyes volleyed back and forth between his parents.

Pierce hemmed, "I was saying—"

"I think it should be the neighbors."

"But—"

"What a perfect way to make up for the noise and flooding your crew caused."

Pierce's nostrils flared as he heaved in a big breath. "All right, June." They whistled when he exhaled. "We'll have the neighbors."

"Good."

"Neighbors?" Brandon asked.

"You'll get your party."

My party? June knew what Pierce was up to. "I couldn't take all the credit. This has got to be our party. We don't have the time or money for more than one this summer."

"I want a party," Nicki repeated.

"Your mother and I are having a party, not you."

"I think—"

"Nicki!" June and Pierce barked in unison.

Cussing under her breath, Nicki stormed toward her

bedroom. Nobody stopped her.

"Fine, June." Pierce stood. "Start making plans."

June couldn't believe it had happened. Her precious dinner, so well-intended, so lovingly prepared, had reverted to dinners like too many others of their recent past. She lumbered over to the phone table. "There was a call for you before dinner," she lifted the message pad and read, "Hugh Sloan. What is he, some newspaper guy?"

"Hugh? He's business agent from the local plumber's Union."

"I would have told you right away, but I didn't know who he was."

"I negotiated the tripartite agreement with him and—"

"And he's rude."

"Only when he's mad." Pierce moved toward the basement door. "I better see what he wants."

"We going swimmin' again, Dad?"

"Maybe later, son."

Nicki's panicked reflex of throwing her diary in the wastebasket the other day was more histrionics than genuine change. Her mother quit emptying her garbage months ago. So until Nicki dumped the contents herself, Leda wasn't going anywhere.

Her initial fear now subsided, Nicki re-read her diary to see what truths about her had been discovered. She found references to her drinking, skipping school to spend a day at Camp Dearborn, a word-for-word recounting of what lies she told her parents before sneaking off to Cedar Point with Nelson and Candy.

Knowing someone had read her most intimate secrets made Nicki want to rip out the pages and shred them into little pieces. But her anger melted from the fire of a delectable plan.

If somebody wants to read my diary, I'll give 'em something to read.

> *Dear Leda,*
>
> *It's official. I'm the class whore. When Candy told me the other day that she slept with our first string quarterback, I knew I couldn't let her win. After all, we had a pact not to sleep with anybody while we were in school. Then she went and screwed the biggest bragger at D.C.*
>
> *Now I'm ahead. I snuck out last night to party with friends, and while a bunch of us were taking hits off one joint after another, I felt the guy next to me rubbing his knee against my thigh. Candy was sitting across from me, and she saw it, too. Every time he did it, she looked at me and giggled. I thought, Okay, pact breaker. Watch this. Then I turned and laid one on him right there in front of everybody. I didn't even know the guy.*
>
> *He says to me "Hey pretty young thing."*
>
> *And I says "Hey back" and everybody laughed.*
>
> *"We have to hang with the children all*

night?" he asks.

I says "My babysitting days ended with Girl Scouts."

Then he took my hand and led me to the bedroom at the back of the house. We did it. Right there with all those people in the other room.

If Candy tries to outdo that, I've got other plans already. I saw Bob & Carol & Ted & Alice, you know.

N

Sneak in here and read that, Nicki smirked and replaced Leda in her nightstand.

Pierce made the call from his basement office. "Hugh? It's Pierce."

"What the hell happened? You've got no Union plumbers in Oshkosh building the modules."

"Of course we do, Hugh. That was our contract."

"Don't I know it. If I hadn't agreed to let you build the modules in Oshkosh, you wouldn't have gotten The Morgan Company's backing in the first place. My Union guys gave up work so you could build in Oshkosh. How could you do it, Pierce? I trusted you."

"Hugh, you know me. I would never—"

"Then you musta got lazy."

"No. I've been at the plant every other week. I was there Friday and saw Union labels on every module in production."

"That's another thing. I'd like to know who got those."

"What are you saying, Hugh?"

"Pierce, I've got proof that you didn't use Union help on the modules. You of all people know better than to screw with the Unions."

"I don't understand."

"Understand this: The Holiday Inn project is shut down. My guys aren't going to touch any modules on the job site or any new ones coming in until you can prove that they're all Union built. If you don't come up with some proof, you're pulling the plumbing tree out of every damn module and having them reinstalled by my field Union tradesmen. You got me?"

Pierce sawed the corner of his mouth with his finger. This wasn't happening. "There must be some miscommunication. Please, Hugh, let me find out what I can."

"You'd better."

"I will. I promise you. There's got to be an explanation for this."

After Pierce hung up, his mind spun every possible scenario for who in The Morgan Company might gain from bypassing the Union in Wisconsin. No one at the top would. Though The American Company investment might seem minuscule compared to their net worth, the investment in the project promised a hearty pay off. No one who stood to gain so much would take such a calculated, or even careless, shortcut. This had to be a mistake.

Pierce looked at the clock. Not yet 6:00. Offices in the central time zone would still be buzzing. He phoned Lenny

Gordon, executive vice president in Oshkosh with whom he had negotiated the Union agreement.

"Good afternoon, Lenny Gordon's office."

"Karen, hi, this is Pierce Humphry. May I speak with Lenny?"

"I'm sorry, Mr. Humphry, but Mr. Gordon left early today." Her granite delivery worried Pierce. He always had a warm rapport with Karen.

Pierce tried to sound unconcerned. "Do you know where I can reach him?"

"I—I really don't know."

It was a lie. She always knew where to find him. Oh, God, thought Pierce, something is very, very wrong.

When Amil Nerus returned the refilled gas can, Mark could hardly mask his excitement.

"It got the job done," said Amil. "I'm only sorry I took so long to bring the can back. To be honest, I forgot about it until I started mowing my back yard."

But Mark wanted to keep him near, if only for a few minutes. "Did you see our pool?"

"I haven't."

"Let me show you." Before Amil could object, Mark led him through the gate.

Solemnly Amil crouched at the edge of the pool and swirled the water with his hand. Blades of grass that had clung to Amil's sweaty arm dipped from the motion then pierced the surface. Seeing them broke Amil's reverential thought. He scooped them up and flung them over the fence.

Passion for this beautiful man left Mark hungering to offer something that would connect them. He smiled, "My parents are planning a pool party for you. The neighbors, I mean."

"Is that right? My girls love to swim."

"No," he waved an open hand self-consciously. "It's for grown ups. Do you swim?" Just picturing Amil in the water excited Mark.

"Mrs. Nerus doesn't. But I love to swim. A party? Good. We look forward to it." He gave the pool area one more approving glance. "Thanks," he smiled.

As Amil left, Mark felt riveted. He had done something good for someone wonderful as Amil.

Chapter

11

June was having her morning tea when Nicki barreled into the kitchen and dropped her fringed purse on the table.

"Where are you going so early?"

"Shopping. Don't worry, friends are picking me up." Nicki pulled out a mirror and lip balm.

"You shouldn't have come home late the night after he took the car away. He'd have given it back by now."

Instead of responding, Nicki closed her lips around a tissue then looked at the imprint they made.

June stared at her daughter. Her long brown hair, tousled now, was nothing like the fine blonde strands that June loved brushing when Nicki was little. June couldn't comprehend why someone as pretty as Nicki would jeopardize her looks to the ravages of late nights and wild antics.

"What is it you find so interesting?" snarled Nicki.

"Nothing."

She shrugged. "Can you drive me to work tomorrow?"

"I—" June didn't know what to say. "I'll have to ask

your father."

"It's a simple question. Can you or can't you?"

June stared into her teacup.

"Fine. I'll find a ride. Thanks for nothing."

"Nicki?" June's tone was so sad, Nicki looked up.

"How do you do it?"

She crinkled her brow. "Do what?"

"How do you...think of yourself..." She groped to finish the question in the right spirit. ". . . just like that?"

The sincerity of June's plea eluded Nicki. "Don't even start. It's bad enough with Dad. I don't need you against me, too."

Before June could reframe her question, Nicki flung her purse over her shoulder and headed out the back door.

"This was not about you," she whispered. The thick ease of slipping back into her murky abyss made June fear she might not have the strength to struggle back out.

"No!" she stood so fast tea splashed out of the cup. She couldn't let it happen. She had to do something.

I'll leave, June decided. Instantly she knew she wasn't ready for that. But even a single step helped stave off another tar pit plummet.

June went downstairs to find a piece of luggage. She grabbed a yellow overnight bag that they'd taken on their honeymoon, but just gripping the handle brought a rush of sentiment that weakened her resolve. She exchanged that piece for an avocado cosmetic case. It would do.

June raced up the stairs and made it all the way to her bedroom unseen. Packing was easy. Not much could fit in the small, box-like case. She tossed in a nightgown, undergarments, a change of clothes, her $2.00 pair of K-Mart Keds. She tucked her mother's rosary into the inside pouch.

What else? She rummaged through her purse for ideas. Sen-Sen, lipstick, Bufferin, Max Factor, tissues, one of Brandon's Hot Wheels, and her "Kiss me, I'm Polish" change purse. June dumped its contents onto the bed: one St. Christopher medal; a loose S & H Green Stamp, two crumpled dollar bills; and 50, 70, 85, 86 cents in change.

June dug out the St. Linus Credit Union ledgers from her lingerie drawer. One for Veronica Lynn, one for Marcus James, one for Brandon Paul. June didn't even have her own account. Whenever she received money, she bought something for the house. Anything left over went toward the kids' savings. "I've got nothing."

Gathering the change from her bed reminded her. Somewhere in the attic she had a glass bank of silver pennies she and her Jaja had saved during the War.

"Wartosc ich bedzie duzo w pryszlym czosie," Jaja promised.

"Worth a lot? How much is a lot?" she asked in broken Polish.

He could not give a figure, but he assured they would be worth bardzo, very much. Finally June could quantify their value. They were worth her salvation.

The attic's only entrance was through the ceiling of Nicki's bedroom closet. June cleared a space on the closet shelf, popped the access panel, and climbed up. She grabbed the flashlight they always left beside the access frame, and scanned the area past the boxes of holiday ornaments and baby clothes. A glass arc glistened through a puff of gray insulation.

June crept along the rafters and retrieved her bank.

The globe was smaller than she remembered, but gripping it in one hand was empowering. Holding her money, she finally felt in control of something.

Leaving Nicki's room, June was so intent on not being heard, she didn't notice one string of beads caught between the frame and door. As she attempted to shut it, one strand broke and beads scattered down the hall.

Just then, the front door opened. Frantically, June scooped up beads.

"Hey! Who's in my room?" Nicki rounded the corner. "You?" she blanched.

A car horn sent Nicki dashing for the wallet she'd forgotten then out the door again.

June added the bank to her cosmetic case, then stuffed it behind the spare tire in the Mercury trunk.

Pierce spent the morning trying to contact Lenny Gordon, whose evasion confirmed Pierce's worst fears. Somebody from The Morgan Company let their own guys do the plumbing. It couldn't have been an innocent mistake. Everyone down to the plant foreman knew the terms of the Union agreement.

Who would violate it? Morgan execs wouldn't risk losing this entire Holiday Inn job. So who would gain from bypassing the Union? Only a plant manager wanting to increase the bottom line for his own profit sharing.

If Howard Creep had done that, then where would Gordon have gone? He'd be in Chicago talking to his labor attorneys.

Pierce tried another tactic for the Chicago call. "Good morning, Loretta, this is Pierce Humphry. I missed my plane and can't get there till this afternoon. Is Lenny Gordon there yet?"

"Yes, sir. He and Mr. Creep arrived over an hour ago."

Pierce scraped the corner of his mouth till it bled. "Tell Lenny I'm waiting to hear from him."

That afternoon, Lenny Gordon returned Pierce's call.

Pierce laid out the information as Hugh Sloan had explained it, then added, "I'll meet you there at your attorney's office tomorrow morning. I want to know what happened and how this mess can be resolved."

Until he met with Gordon, Pierce could accomplish nothing except getting his ticket to Chicago. He couldn't even field calls. If this debacle did end up in court, his misinformation could work against him. Throughout the day, Linda took messages from irate hotel executives and contractors who wanted answers now. Pierce did, too.

As dinner began, Mark noted a silence among the dinnertime grapplers cool enough to frost their iced tea glasses. For a change, Nicki's icy stares were directed toward their mother, whose stoic indifference gave her an angelic glow. His dad, on the other hand, was sallow as a corpse.

"June," he began, "I've been re-thinking the pool party with the neighbors."

You gotta have the party, Mark pleaded in his mind, I already told Amil, and he was so happy.

Brandon blurted, "I wanna have a party."

"Oh eat your vegetables," June instructed, not taking her eyes from Pierce. "No party?"

"Not yet. Let's wait...till...later."

"And instead of neighbors, how about family?"

Mark interjected. "But the neighbors would be so excited."

"We can think about it," Pierce offered. "Later."

"But you already said you were going to invite the neighbors."

"So we changed our minds," his father said.

"But—"

"No harm done."

"But—"

Brandon looked up. "Oh eat your vegetables." And everyone laughed, except Mark.

It isn't fair, he thought. Poor Amil was being uninvited to something that had been promised him. What do I tell him now?

As he washed the dishes that night, Mark struggled to form just the right apology. He wanted to be sincere, yet strong. Even after he finished the dishes and joined his dad and Brandon in the pool, he still didn't know what to say.

"Let's play Commando," Brandon, already a good enough swimmer to forego his life jacket, paddled toward his father.

"Tonight, son?"

"Come on, Dad. I can get across this time. Lemme try."

Brandon's objective was to slink into the water, swim silently across the pool, then emerge without being heard. If Pierce, eyes closed and back to Brandon, heard him splash, he could yell "target detected" and Brandon lost the game. If he made it across unnoticed, Brandon won the war and became a hero.

While Brandon and Pierce played Commando, Mark reenacted the underwater scenes of *The Poseidon Adventure* by pulling himself along the rope that divided the shallow and deep ends of the pool. The role-playing dulled his concern for Amil only momentarily. Mark wanted to do right by Amil, whose brief attention made Mark hunger for more.

Next time I see him, I'll set things right, Mark decided.

With that thought, Mark turned to see Amil standing at the gate in a ragged T-shirt and cut-offs. The image revived the hard-work scent that Amil carried and instantly excited Mark. He couldn't get out of the water and correct his mistake now.

Amil approached Pierce who stood at the far end of the pool, arms folded over the edge. "Pierce, you all right?" Amil apparently didn't even notice Mark.

"Playing Commando," Pierce whispered and pointed to Brandon sneaking across the water.

In silence Pierce, Mark and Amil waited for Brandon to

reach the other side. When he made it without Pierce yelling "Target detected," Brandon raised his arms victoriously.

"I did it, didn't I? I did it."

Then he saw his father, brother and neighbor looking at him. "You didn't yell 'Target detective' like you were 'posed to," he pouted. "I thought I did it."

"You did, son."

"I wanted to win," he swam to the shallow end to play alone.

"Was this my fault?" Amil asked.

"No, no. He's fine."

As Pierce emerged from the water Amil protested, "Please, don't get out. I borrowed some gas to finish mowing my lawn. I refilled the can and returned it yesterday, but I wanted to thank you in person."

"Sure. Glad we could help." Pierce dried himself off. "Have you seen the pool all completed?"

"As a matter of fact I was here yesterday, with Mark."

"I'm proud of this pool," Pierce offered.

"You should be. What you've achieved!"

Pierce's face paled, but he continued. "The kids already love it, and June and I will get our share of pleasure from it, too. We'll probably end up having a party."

Amil smiled expectantly.

"For our family."

The phrase eclipsed his bright expression. "Family?"

"Yeah, we didn't do much to celebrate Mark's graduation from St. Linus, so we thought we might have some of June's and my relatives over for a pool party."

It's a lie, thought Mark. But even after Amil left, Mark still couldn't find words to heal the hurt he'd caused. Some day I will fix this for you. Mark jumped out of the pool and wrapped a towel around him to hide the evidence of his excitement.

"Where're you going?" Brandon asked.

"In."

Mark locked the bedroom door and peeled off his trunks. A hungry thrill shot through him.

He lay on his bed, eyes closed. "Amil," he whispered just to hear the name from his own voice.

Heat jolted through him as images of Amil surfaced and grew more precise, more immediate: The curve of Amil's veined forearm. Amil kneeling over him after the accident. His sweet inquiry. The attention from his deep set eyes.

Thoughts raced and pounded.

Amil's broad, angular shoulders, legs solid and shapely as he knelt by the pool. Dark shaded knees, the sleek line of his shin.

Images sped. Mark saw everything. Amil's hair, eyes, smile, teeth, chest, fingers, thighs, feet, skin.

"Amil." Mark whispered breathlessly. "Help me." Sensations teased, pounded, exploded.

Then, stillness.

When Mark opened his eyes, his isolation felt comfortable. He took a long shower, then stayed in for the night.

"You feeling all right?" his mother asked him as they watched TV.

He answered, "Yes," but wasn't sure what he felt.

After she caught June sneaking out of her room, Nicki didn't know who was reading her diary. Though still convinced it was her father, she now had evidence against her mom.

They must both be in on it, she decided. And any parents who would read their daughter's diary deserve what I'm doing.

As Nicki wrote more lies in Leda, frustration with her parents escalated to fury. Just thinking about their betrayal reminded Nicki of a photograph she once saw in *Life* magazine. Beside an article about Kent State, the photo contained a cluster of irate students. Arms and legs and screaming faces surrounded one student in the center of the picture, his arm thrust forward flipping the bird with such rage, Nicki swore she saw his nerve endings shooting out of this body.

She became so riled just remembering this picture that she couldn't continue the story she'd begun in tonight's entry. Instead she just wrote, "Kent State, Kent State, Kent State," all the way down the page. Rather than signing off with her initial, she drew a hand with the middle finger raised.

Chapter

12

Arriving in Chicago with his lawyer, Seymour Rosenthal, Pierce felt doom shadowing him like an assassin. His fear revived the most contemptible memory of his childhood: the Friend-of-the-Court. Every man he passed at the airport, on the road, in the parking lot of Blanchart, Brookman, & Meyer looked like him. Every sound echoed with his heavy footsteps on the cement stairs beyond their front door.

"Mom, he's here," young William Pierce would rush to the kitchen and whisper, then run back to the front of the house, swiping dust off the end table before opening the door.

"Hello, young man."

Pierce detested the fake congeniality of the fat intruder.

"I'm here for our visit. Is your mother even home?" he asked, as if trying to catch them in violation of the law.

After Pierce's father left, Betta became unflappable. She never flinched when borrowing money from her socialite sister just to pay the mortgage. With no experience, she secured an assembly line position at Bulldogs Factory on her first day job hunting. She even convinced her chauvinist brother-in-law to teach her how to buy a car on her own.

She easily swallowed her pride about everything except the court order that assumed a divorced woman couldn't raise her own child without being held legally accountable. Nothing fazed her, except the Friend-of-the-Court and his surprise inspections.

Young Pierce sensed his mother's fear of this odious man. Though she was always a tidy housekeeper, never knowing when he might drop by made her obsessive. Each morning before heading to work, she left Pierce an exhaustive list of chores. He faithfully completed them until the day he lost track of time listening to *I Love a Mystery*.

His rapt attention was interrupted by the rag man's horse clip-clopping down the alley behind their house. Though he seemed to cause no one harm just hollering, "rags, rags" and rummaging through garbage, rumors abounded that he kidnapped little children.

Instantly Pierce became Jack from *I Love a Mystery*. He devised his mission to save the children who must be trapped under the old newspapers piled in the back of the rag man's buckboard wagon. He was flying off the fence onto the imaginary villain when his mother arrived home. Not one of the chores had even been started.

She screamed for him to come in from the back yard and ranted about each item on the list, then continued, "Do you understand why the Friend-of-the-Court inspects our house? Do you know what he has the power to do? That fat man with the wrinkled suit and scuffed shoes can decide in a single visit whether you can live here or not. Don't you know the only hope we have is to keep this place looking like a palace in some movie? I need you to help me."

Before she could finish, Pierce was crying. She pulled him toward her and consumed him in a tearful embrace. "I don't want you to go to an orphanage. I don't want to lose you."

That night Pierce acquired his own obsession. Every day for the rest of his adolescence he kept the house meticulous. As an adult, Pierce's penchant for perfection translated into his work. It made facing this challenge even more unfathomable.

Lenny Gordon was not alone with the senior partner when Pierce and Seymour arrived. Howard Creep was in the conference room, too.

Maintaining his composure, Pierce tolerated a few minutes of congenial gladhanding by Morgan Company attorney John Holden before succinctly encapsulating what he knew.

Holden fielded Pierce's questions and remained blithely evasive until Pierce bottom lined it. "The Unions say that their plumbers didn't work on the modules. If they didn't, who did?"

"Union guys did work on 'em," Howard insisted.

"Howard," John silenced him.

"My Union guys say they have proof that somebody violated the agreement. It wasn't The American Company. So what happened?"

"It's your job, Pierce. You tell us."

"I'm in Detroit. I come to Oshkosh nearly every other

week to check progress on the modules. When I visit, everything looks in order. The Union seals are even affixed where they should be. Then I get a call from the BA in Detroit that his Union guy was let go and the work proceeded. First, that's not the agreement that I worked my ass off to secure. Second, if the Detroit Union guy was let go, somebody got rid of him, and somebody else did the work. Who? Who? Who?"

"It was Union." Howard boomed.

"But what Union?"

"What difference does it make?"

"All the difference. The Detroit Unions only let us build in Oshkosh if their guys did the final connections. You knew that, Howard."

"But Union is Union. What if the Detroit guy didn't show and my guys are there waiting on his lazy ass? My men are Millman Union. You saying they couldn't do the job good as he could?"

"Howard!" John snapped.

"Not according to the Union agreement."

"Union is Union. What's the difference?"

"Oh, Howard," Pierce dropped back in his chair. "You know the difference. The agreement was for these specific Union people to work their trades. In signing the agreement, the Detroit Union gave up valuable work to let the modules be built in Oshkosh. Why do you think they're so irate? Can you blame them for shutting down the job?"

"Your Union can't stop our job," Lenny interrupted, "That's a secondary boycott."

"They've done it, and apparently with good cause. So

what do we do now?"

"We?" John asked.

"Howard just admitted—"

"He asked a few hypothetical questions. We don't know anything more than you do. If the Detroit Union has a beef, it's against The American Company."

"If the job doesn't get up and running again quickly—"

"I see your concern," John offered condescendingly. "You'll have lawsuits coming at you from every direction. Including ours."

Seymour stood. "We understand. Thanks for your time."

"No. I want answers," Pierce demanded. "There were Detroit Union seals on my modules every time I came by to check them. If your guys were doing the work, how'd you get the seals, Howard? Did you pay the guy off? Did you steal them?"

John stepped toward the door.

"And how long have you been getting away with it? Did you know every time I came by and asked you to your face how things were going?"

Seymour squeezed Pierce's arm. "Come on, Pierce."

"What were you thinking as I praised you for the work you were doing every other God damn week for the last—"

"Pierce," Seymour whispered.

Pierce got to his feet. "No, I want to know. By God if I lose everything for one son-of-a-bitch laborer's profit share cut, I have a right to know when and how it happened. Howard, are you man enough to tell me how you screwed my company, how you kicked to death a lifetime of work?"

"Pierce," Seymour guided Pierce out of the office.

"You got me by the balls here, Howard. You enjoying the grip? You and the guys can have a good laugh over this one in the breakroom, 'eh Howard? You worked my little company over but good, didn't you? Where's your bottom line now that the job's shut down? Was it worth it?" Pierce yelled down the hall. "By God, you're not rid of me yet. If you think so, you don't know Pierce Humphry."

Mark woke that morning devastated by one thought: If Amil knew what I was feeling, he would hate me. Yet Mark's affection was so exciting and beautiful, he couldn't deny it. Instead, he determined to protect it. I won't share my feelings, Mark concluded, not with Amil, not with anyone.

That afternoon when Russell came over to swim, Mark tested his new resolve.

Russell approach on his Schwinn Heavy Duty. "Hi."

"Hi."

"What's the matter with you?"

"Nothing. Why?"

"Nothing, I guess."

There was a lull.

"What?"

"You seem different."

It's working, Mark thought. "Different?"

"I don't know. You're acting weird."

"Weird?"

"Different."

Mark was pleased. "You ready to swim?"

Russell followed Mark around the house and past the Nerus's yard. In her bathing suit, eldest daughter Kim watered the plants separating their two properties.

"Hey, you going swimming?"

Mark stopped on the pathway, but didn't move any closer to her.

"It sure is a hot day." She turned the water hose and sprayed her heavy legs.

"Yeah," Mark took another step toward the pool area.

"Don't you think it's hot?" Kim blurted at Russell to keep them from dismissing her. "I feel like I'm on fire." She moved the hose upward and let it pour over her chest. "Whew," she sighed. "I can't stand it." She shot the water straight down her cleavage. After a dramatic pause, she moaned, "Oh, even that doesn't help...not enough."

When she pulled the water hose away, her bathing suit clung to her pancake stack rolls of fat, huge breasts, and pointed nipples. Russell and Mark stared, but avoided looking at one another for fear they would burst out laughing right in front of her. With no gracious way out, Mark finally said, "I'll ask my dad if you guys can come swimming some time."

She dropped the hose and started toward the house. "I'll go get everybody."

"Not today," Mark stopped her. "I can't ask him today. He's out of town."

"When will he be back?"

"Tonight some time."

Reluctantly Kim picked up the hose again. "Yeah, well, maybe tomorrow."

Mark led Russell to the pool area. Safely beyond the six foot fence, both boys looked at each other and began snickering so loud they had to jump in and finish laughing underwater so they wouldn't be heard.

As they treaded water Mark thought how comfortable he was around Russell. Except for Mark's interest in *The Poseidon Adventure*, Russell actually knew very little about him. Good thing, Mark thought.

"Let's do the underwater scenes."

"I'm Gene Hackman."

"I know," Russell rolled his eyes, "You're always Gene Hackman."

That left the Shelley Winters part to Russell. Mark was relieved. Today he couldn't have stood playing a female.

As Russell hopped out of the pool, Mark sat at the edge of the water beside the rope dividing the deep and shallow ends. "We can do it," Mark began, "Believe me we can do it." He pretended to tie a rope around his waist. "I'm gonna swim through. I'll tie the rope on the other end. When I get there, I'll give you a tug, a'right? The rest of you pull yourself along the rope. Take a deep breath first. It can't be more than thirty seconds at the most."

"Mister Scott, how long can you hold your breath?" Russell knelt beside Mark, waddling a bit in his best imitation of an overweight matron.

"I don't know."

"All right, do me a favor, please. Try it, now. Mr. Rogo, time him."

Russell extended an imaginary chai medal in front of Mark. "Mr. Scott, look at this. Look. I was the underwater swimming champ of New York, three years running. I held my breath two minutes and forty-seven seconds. Let me do this, please."

Russell skipped some dialogue to continue Winters' speech. "Oh, for hours you've all been dragging and pulling me all this way. Now I have a chance to do something I know how to do. Please, may I do this for everybody?"

"Mrs. Rosen, I think I'm perfectly capable of holding my breath long enough to swim thirty-five feet." Mark felt a sudden sinking in his chest as he looked at Russell. Hackman's next action was to cup his hands around Winters' cheeks and thank her with a kiss. Russell saved the situation by grabbing a bottle of suntan oil and handing it to Mark with a heavy Ernest Borgnine inflection. "Hey, preacher."

Mark took the imaginary flashlight, held his breath in puffed out cheeks, then slipped into the pool. Underwater, Mark twisted through the invisible ship's wreckage and pretended the safety ladder was the one Hackman passed to enter the ship's next chamber.

Mark came up for air before heading back to the bottom of the deep end. He spread his arms and dropped his flashlight as if pinned by the steel panel.

On cue, Russell dove right in, pulled himself along the rope dividing both sides of the pool, then made his way toward the trapped preacher.

Engrossed in his role playing, Mark didn't think about

Russell's having to grab him from behind to pull him to the surface. Though Russell merely wrapped his arm around Mark's neck, contact with his skin repulsed Mark so violently he broke the hold with a convulsive elbow jab into Russell's stomach. Springing up for air, Mark shuddered in disgust. He was so pre-occupied with his own reactions he didn't hear the bubbles of Russell's exhaled air rumble as they broke the surface of the water.

Mark barely took time to inhale before jumping out of the pool and wrapping his arms around to his back. He swiped wildly with his fingers. When that brought no relief, he ran to the picnic table where he'd thrown his towel, wound both ends around his fists and scrubbed his back till it stung.

With a final shudder Mark rested his arms and dropped one end of the towel. As it fell at his feet, he sensed a sudden embarrassment. When he turned around, Russell would be staring at him in confusion, expecting an explanation for the strange behavior. Despite a flood of possible excuses, no reasonable lie came to mind. Mark turned. "I just don't want to do this anymo—"

Russell wasn't staring up at him.

"Hey," Mark called, wondering how Russell could have disappeared without being heard.

Mark barely needed one step closer to the deep end to distinguish the dark mass at the bottom of the pool. It was Russell, his body spread and motionless like the corpse in overalls that Shelley Winters swam past before saving Gene Hackman—and meeting her own death immediately after.

In his panic Mark didn't pull Russell from the water.

He called for his mother. "Mom!" He pounded on the glass door. "Help, Mom! Mom!"

"What?!" June's voice boomed through the house even before she appeared. "What's wrong?"

Mark was white with terror.

"My God, what is it?" She scurried down the patio steps.

Motioning toward the pool, Mark knew immediately what he should have done first. He lunged into the water, grabbed Russell by the arm and pulled him to the surface.

At the edge of the pool June grabbed Russell's sallow body from her son. "He's not breathing."

Together, they pulled Russell out of the pool and lay him face up on the concrete. June opened her arms helplessly. "I don't know what to do. What are we gonna do, baby?"

Mark had already leapt to his feet. "Dad!" he hollered toward the still open glass door. "Dad, help!"

"He's not home," June cried, not taking her eyes off Russell. Tentatively, she pushed on his stomach. "Go get help." As Mark disappeared, she opened Russell's mouth then pressed on his abdomen again, watching for water to drain. When nothing happened she pushed rhythmically on his chest.

Mark ran into the Nerus's garage and banged on their door.

"Yas, yas."

"Mrs. Nerus," Mark called as she came into view. "Help us. My friend...at our pool...we can't get him to breathe..."

From over Mrs. Nerus's shoulder, her sleepy, disheveled husband appeared. "What's the problem?"

"Please help us. My friend drowned."

"Chou, call an ambulance," Amil commanded and followed Mark to the pool. June was still trying unsuccessfully to force air into Russell.

"Oh, God, Amil," June gasped. "Help me here. I don't know what I'm doing. Do you know how?"

He knelt and studied Russell with such focus that they didn't hear his muffled "No." Regardless, he pushed down on Russell's jaw and blew two heavy breaths into the inert boy.

"I think we need to count, like one and two, in between."

June echoed a steady "one and two" then watched Amil repeat his attempt with no success.

Mark tried to formulate a coherent prayer, but in his fear and confusion he could only stand out of the way watching Russell's stomach for movement. In nervous agitation Mark looked up. To his surprise Nicki was stepping toward the open glass door. With one glance at the situation, she barreled forward, pushed the adults out of the way, and took charge.

She lifted Russell's shoulders so his head dropped back slightly. With one hand she opened his mouth. With the forefinger of her other, she swiped his throat. Pinching his nose she breathed twice into his mouth, turned her head sideways as she paused and listened, then repeated the motion only twice more before she got the reaction for which they'd all been trying. Russell coughed. Nicki turned him on his side as he vomited. He hacked and moaned, eventually regaining a natural breathing rhythm.

Tears of relief welled in Mark's eyes. June made the sign of the cross. "Thank you, Boza."

Nicki sat back on her heels and looked at her mother. "You should have called me first. Do you think I can't remember anything?"

"I forgot you knew," June told her.

Mark knelt beside Nicki debating whether to apologize to Russell or act confused about what had happened. Saying nothing, he smiled with feigned courage.

June got Pierce's robe from the house and covered Russell with it. Soon he felt stable enough to sit up. Amil remained in the cluster until his wife ran up to say the ambulance was on its way.

As they heard the sirens, Mark knew he had to say something. "I'm sorry."

Russell didn't seem to hear Mark's weak apology.

"Russell," he cleared his throat then looked directly at his friend. "I'm sorry. I don't know what happened."

"Me neither," was Russell's only reply.

On the way home from Chicago, Pierce and Seymour had a few drinks and brainstormed strategies for getting the Union back on the job.

"There's got to be something you can negotiate."

"What do I have to offer? The American Company has no money coming in, and The Morgan Company's not backing me for anything."

"Maybe you can contribute to the Union Welfare Fund once you start generating income again."

"Yes. I could start with that."

"It's something to take to the table."

"An explanation and an offer like that might help. Hugh Sloan knows me. He said himself I'm good for my word."

"But none of the other guys do. And to them, you haven't been."

"You helping me here?"

"I'm just saying you've got to offer them something concrete. Explanations and promises will get you as far as we got today."

Seymour slept the rest of the flight from Chicago O'Hare, but Pierce was too restless. Over Detroit, he looked down at its signature cars buzzing along freeways, racing around ramps, starting and stopping, a frenetic, interwoven symbol of the once opulent and upwardly mobile Motor City.

Peering down at the houses and trees of the west side suburbs, Pierce sought the one glistening speck that rendered him distinguishable amid all the aging images below: his pool. He found it. The kidney shaped sparkle of blue looked like a tailless fish lying docile. It was so beautiful Pierce felt his throat constrict.

Instead of pride or exaltation in the fulfillment of a dream, Pierce only felt his distance from it. Like vertigo, the pool disappeared in a swirl of his peripheral vision behind the edge of the narrow little airplane window. With a single blink it was behind him, completely out of sight.

Pierce was so drained from his Chicago confrontation that finding out about Russell only numbed him further. Before Nicki finished her explanation, Pierce headed to Garden City Hospital and immediately took charge. He got an update from the doctors, assured Russell's mother that everything would be fine, then went to the parking lot and sat with Russell's father until the boy was released and everyone went home.

Driving alone in the car behind June and Mark, Pierce was stung by the ironic timing of Russell's accident. If Russell had drowned, his parents would have sued. On the very day Pierce's business crumbled, a catastrophe instantly could have taken everything the Humphrys had. Instead, he thought, it will soon be bled from us in slow, painful drops.

Chapter

13

This morning especially, Pierce looked forward to his weekly breakfast with his mother. It was his one opportunity to forget his troubles and just be taken care of. As he stopped in her driveway, she peered around the kitchen curtains and waved. She was a tiny woman bent over from an arthritic back. She looked older than her 65 years, testimony to a fighting spirit that had seen its share of lost battles. Drooping skin punctuating the lines of her mouth. There was no mistaking that she and Pierce were mother and son.

Pierce hugged her gently. In summer's humidity her neck was stiff and sore.

"Good morning, son," Betta shuffled over to the same dripolator she'd used for the past thirty years.

"Good morning, mother of mine!" he sat at the dining room table already set for breakfast. He was too jovial to be convincing. This is my mother, he thought, she'll see right through me.

She served him coffee and sat across from him with

keen attention.

Pierce tapped the rim of his saucer.

"You need to trim your fingernails," she said.

He looked at them instead of her. "Mom," he finally offered. "Mom—"

She took a sip of her coffee and waited.

"Nixon's out, isn't he?"

"I don't want to get your hackles up, son, but I've been telling you, you reap what you sow. His bitter harvest has come in."

"But if he didn't do it. If he didn't know but was left with the blame…. I don't know." He threw up his hands. "Seems we've gotten to a point when you can't trust anybody any more."

"You can't stop trusting everybody."

"No, but one bad apple…"

"Or in this case several. But not all."

Pierce paused to consider a moment. "In other cases, just one."

"Sometimes one."

Unwilling to burden her with his troubles, Pierce changed the subject. "There was a little mishap at the pool. Mark's friend, Russell, took in a lung full of water and had to be resuscitated. I wasn't home when it happened, but apparently it was pretty traumatic for him."

"The poor boy. Will he be all right?"

"Oh, yes. He's fine."

"And you?"

"What?"

"Are you all right?"

"How do you mean?"

"Just asking."

"Oh, sure. It could have been very bad, but it wasn't."

"Thanks God for that."

She always added that 's.' Pierce never knew why. "Thank God."

"Yes," she repeated, "Thanks God."

"So, no, I'm fine. It's just been a rough month, I guess. Not just that, but," he took a deep breath and hesitated like a soldier approaching a suspiciously silent war zone, "you know, work. Work's been... tough."

Betta nodded yes and waited for him to continue.

After several more seconds of debating in his mind whether or not to begin, he shook his head and muttered a heart-heavy, "Oh, Mom."

"All right, Pierce, it's time for you to tell me."

He wanted to pour over every detail. Even if she didn't understand the technical aspects, she would recognize his pain and concern. She would take care of him.

But he couldn't do it. Emotion stuck in his Adam's apple and would not pass. Unable to meet her eyes, he looked around the kitchen. On the bureau between her radio and brass lazy susan was a cap.

"Did Brandon leave that here?"

"No," she smiled. "Don't you recognize it?"

As he picked it up, his heart warmed with reminiscence. "Why this is mine. Where did you ever...?"

"I was cleaning out some boxes in the basement and there it was."

"Well I'll be." He fingered it tenderly. This emblem

from their past brought Pierce a new rush of emotion. He could handle his problems alone. He didn't need to burden his mother with them.

Breakfast ended with few words. As Pierce leaned forward to kiss her good-bye, she hugged him tightly. "I love you, William."

He was touched beyond words. He smiled bravely and turned to leave.

"Here, your hat." She handed him his baseball cap.

He looked at it, still speechless.

She rubbed his back as he walked away. "I'll see you next week."

As he headed to his car, Pierce wondered how he could turn and wave goodbye without letting her see how overwrought he was. Then he knew. If he put on the cap, he could make his mother smile. With the brim shading part of his face, Pierce turned around, grinned and waved.

Once inside his car, Pierce recognized a familiar scent that revived feelings of safety and love. He brought the cap to his nostrils and inhaled. It was a blend of talc and the wool of his mother's sweater from so very long ago.

One night in particular came to mind. The Friend-of-the-Court had paid his heinous visit, so his mother had been tense all day. Though it seemed to Pierce the inspection went well, she remained edgy even after the man left. Eventually she told Pierce just to go to bed. She wanted to be alone.

Naturally Pierce couldn't sleep. He kept listening for his mother's movements and watching her shadow interrupt the light beneath his bedroom door. After a long time she entered Pierce's room.

"Son?" she whispered in the sweetest voice he'd ever heard. "I'm sorry."

She lay beside him on his bed and held him tightly. When she squeezed him her rough wool sweater scratched his cheek. He didn't care. He snuggled to her as close as he could and let her hold him in her arms. The scent that reached his nose was talc, but to him it was simply the beautiful, familiar scent of his mother.

Pierce set his cap on the seat beside him. Backing out of his mother's driveway, he was overwhelmed. He drove down her street just far enough to be completely out of view from her house. Then he pulled over to the curb and wept.

Russell rode to Mark's house about 10:00 a.m., this time without a bathing suit and towel. "Hi."

Mark traced his finger along the metal porch railing.

"How do you feel?"

"About what?"

Mark frowned.

"Oh. Fine. I just think I've had enough Poseidon Adventuring for awhile."

Mark now found everything about Russell irksome: his broad frame, his chubby body, his slumping posture. If what his father once said were true, and his choice in friends really was an indication of what he thought of himself, then everything Mark now saw in Russell blared "not much, not much."

Nevertheless, Mark blamed himself for what happened at the pool. Despite his need for emotional distance, he still cared enough about Russell to make amends for the terrible mishap that nearly cost his friend's life.

"I'm really sorry about what happened."

"Why did you do it?"

Fear coursed through Mark. "Do what?"

"The reflex. You hit me or kicked me or something."

"I don't know," he shuddered at the memory of Russell's skin against his own.

"You lie."

"I don't know," he blurted, "but I am sorry, and I said so."

"Okay," growled Russell. Then he softened, "It is okay."

Trusting Russell's sincerity, Mark felt absolved, though he still was unwilling to forgive himself. "Thanks."

"Your sister's pretty good. I guess I ought to thank her."

Mark rose with a quick, "I'll get her," and rushed into the house.

At Nicki's closed bedroom door Mark breathed deeply. He needed a break from Russell. Finally he tapped on her door. "Nick?"

"Mark?"

"It's me, yeah."

She opened the door. In her orange ruffled shorty pajamas she looked like the young Nicki who used to talk him into playing Barbies with her.

"Russell's outside. He wants to thank you."

Her brows dipped curiously. Mark guessed it had been a quite a while since anyone had noticed anything good she'd done, and even longer since someone took the time to tell her.

"Let me get some clothes on."

Like everything he did, Russell expressed his gratitude with directness and precision. "You know you saved my life," he said, more like a paramedic than an accident victim. "I guess I won't ever know exactly how it happened," Russell kept his sincere gaze on Nicki, "but I'm sure you're the one who saved me. The doctor said so, my parents know so. My mom came to my hospital bed and had us pray. First thing she did after thanking God for my life was to thank Him for you. You don't know my mother, but that's something. So," Russell relaxed his shoulders conclusively, "thank you."

Nicki beamed. "I never thought my little brother would end up having a cool friend, but you're all right."

Once Nicki was back in the house, Mark had no idea what to say. He felt foolish and immature. Inexplicably his sister now seemed all right herself. But Russell talked with her like someone too mature to play Poseidon Adventure or sneak off to smoke cigarettes. Mark was confused. One minute he thought he was too good to hang around a tubby, goofy guy like Russell. The next, he felt unworthy of his friendship.

Either way, they couldn't stay friends. Russell knew him too well. He would eventually figure things out. He already suspected something about the swimming mishap.

It was all too much for Mark. He wanted to hide.

"Are you gonna sit there all day and say nothing?" Russell asked.

"I might."

He winced. "What's the matter with you?"

"Nothing." Normally Mark would have suggested they just go find something to do, but no words came. He could feel himself slipping back into obscurity and liking the ease of not fighting it.

"What do you want to do?"

"I don't know," Mark offered with a resignation that was as close to a brush-off as he could muster.

"Think of something."

Mark shrugged.

"You wanna go smoke?" asked Russell.

"Do you have cigarettes?"

"No, but I've got money. I'll buy 'em."

"You really want to?"

"I don't mind."

If he weren't so accommodating, this would be easy, Mark thought. But as Russell waited patiently for a reply, Mark began to doubt that getting rid of him was really what he wanted to do. After all, there was comfort in the familiar. Russell was definitely that.

They rode together to P & L Market on Hass. Waiting outside with the bikes while Russell went in, Mark peeked through the security bars at the leather-faced woman.

Instead of going directly to the cigarettes, Russell walked over to the candy counter.

"Just pick what you want and buy it. You wanna

browse, go to Sears."

Russell grabbed some Pixie Sticks and $100,000 Bar, then picked up a copy of *Nation's Business* and dropped it face up beside the register. "My dad also wants a pack of Pall Mall."

Her layered eyelids fluttering, the old woman squinted at the magazine then up at Russell doubtfully.

"I'm gonna eat this now," he showed her a Pixie Stick. Then he tore off the tip and, like a polite boy, placed it in the small sack for paper and bottle caps beside the register. Tilting his head back, he poured the flavored granules into his mouth.

She rang up the purchase and tossed the pack of cigarettes in the bag.

"Thank you," Russell waved as he left the store. "Piece of cake," he told Mark when the door closed behind him.

Kinloch Park was teeming with noisy kids so Mark and Russell changed their plans and rode over to Municipal Park near city hall and the Caroline Kennedy Library. To get there, they passed Haston, the public junior high growing infamous for its drug problems. Seeing the school reminded Mark that they were only weeks away from starting high school at Divine Child. Not having to go to Crestwood, the public high school where students went after Haston, didn't alleviate Mark's dread.

A double-tiered rocket slide dominated the now quiet Municipal Park. Mark and Russell leaned against an ivy covered fence and lit their cigarettes.

"Have you ever been inside Haston? Or Crestwood?"

"Oh, sure," laughed Mark.

With menacing sincerity, the St. Linus nuns always warned them to avoid Haston where, they claimed, rough students grabbed St. Linus kids, took them behind the school and forced them to smoke little sticks that made them crazy.

Those stories stopped abruptly when the Catholic schools in the Detroit area faced financial setbacks and had to raise tuition. The crunch intensified when nationally respected Sacred Heart High School closed altogether, limiting the space elsewhere. As a result competition to attend the remaining campuses increased. Some schools even had to reject new students who'd already received letters of acceptance.

"I have," said Russell.

"What?"

"Been inside Crestwood."

"Sure."

"I have...with my mother."

"Yeah," Mark scoffed.

"For freshman registration."

Everything got so still even the flies stopped buzzing around them.

Not knowing what to say, Mark held his cigarette between his lips. He finally exhaled, "Sure."

"I knew you wouldn't like it, but how do you think I feel?"

"I don't know." Mark was drowning once again in the same anxiety he felt at graduation. Now his fear was compounded by the thought of facing a new school without his only friend.

"Not good, all right?" Russell said.

"Why?"

"Why don't I feel good?"

"Why aren't you going to Divine Child? You were accepted. I saw the letter."

"One of 'em."

Mark didn't understand.

"Another letter came later. Enrollment ran over because of Sacred Heart."

"I didn't get a letter, and your grades are better than mine."

"You also have a sister already going to D.C."

Mark pressed his cigarette into the ground. "I need to go," his voice quivered. He hopped on his bike and rode away.

Mark refused to cry. He was a man now, and he was determined to act like one. As he circled the court, he saw Amil and felt nothing for him. "Good," he thought. He screeched to a halt and threw his bike on the garage floor. "To hell with everybody." He bounded into the house.

That evening, Toke picked up Nicki on his Harley. She didn't invite him in or introduce him to her mom and dad, but she felt their steely eyes watching her as she rode away.

Nicki treated Toke to some White Castle burgers on the way to his apartment. As they continued making jewelry, Nicki described her rescue. "My mother, Mark, and the neighbor guy were just kneeling there looking at him. I plowed right through and resuscitated the kid."

"Bomb."

"It was a wild scene, but I did it. I saved that boy's life."

"I said, 'Bomb.'"

"Really it was. I wasn't scared or anything. I knew what to do and didn't think twice about taking it on—even when all the adults were totally freaked."

"Hand me the torch."

"They ended up taking Russell to Garden City." Nicki continued as Toke welded a clasp onto a necklace. "But they didn't have to keep him overnight or anything. I revived him in plenty of time. I did everything just right."

"Hm."

"And you know what else? Russell came over today and thanked me for his life. It was so cool. He just called me out to the porch and said that his mother was so grateful to me she cried."

"Look," he held up his newest creation.

"She cried," Nicki repeated, "because I saved her son's life."

"Try it on."

"Did you hear me?"

"I got it, I got it. You did a good thing." He studied the necklace design. "Add some blue shading to that. You got some blue there?"

"Yeah," she stirred the paint and continued working in silence.

After 11:00, Nicki closed the paint jars and stretched. "I work in the morning, remember?"

"I told you I'd take you. You want to just stay here?"

The suggestion surprised Nicki. "No, I need to get home."

Toke dropped her off well before curfew. She peered into her parent's room and found her dad already in bed. "I'm home."

"Nicki?"

"Yeah. I'm early."

"Good. What time do you work tomorrow?"

"Eight."

"We need to leave by 7:40 then?"

"No, thanks. I've got a ride." She closed the door and got ready for bed.

Chapter

14

Saturday mornings were always busy. Nicki had gone to work, Pierce was out mowing the lawn while Mark edged, and June had errands to run. Normally she didn't mind going alone. But Russell's pool incident scared June right out of her withdrawal and left her hungering for human contact.

"Brandon, honey," June turned down the television volume. "You want to go with Mama?"

"Mark will."

"He's doing the lawn with Dad. You don't want to be in the house by yourself."

"It's cartoons."

"Okay, but don't sit so close to the TV. You'll strain your eyes."

"Bring me candy."

"Not if you're not going with me."

"Please. And Wacky Packs."

At her first stop, June didn't dash out of the cleaners as usual. She indulged old Cora who repeated the same story about her gall bladder attack every time June came in.

June tried to strike up a conversation with the young clerk at Tele-Warren Bakery, but the bread slicer was loud and a line of people waited behind her.

In Kowalski's, June knew the woman behind the counter with the crooked smile and ashen fillings in her teeth. "And how are things for you?" June asked before selecting her lunch meat.

"You're in a good mood today."

"I'll take a pound of this ham and that hard salami, sliced thin for sandwiches. I'm all right. You having a good morning?"

"Fair. Bologna's on sale. Pound of that, too?"

"I'll take half a pound."

"Your son hasn't been coming with you lately."

"Who Mark? He's starting high school in the fall. Divine Child."

"They outgrow us faster'n their clothes." She finished slicing. "Anything else?"

"Oh, yeah, fill a small candy bag with Mary Janes, Squirrels, and Bit-O-Honey. And give me one Wacky Pack."

June passed through the produce department in Danny's just as a stocker opened a fresh box of Red Delicious apples. The scent stopped June in her tracks. "Jaja." She closed her eyes and inhaled.

"Lady, you all right?"

June's eyes shot open. "Yes," she smiled. "I'm fine. I'm going home."

June had never driven all the way from Dearborn Heights to Hamtramck by herself. But with an excited resolve, she headed to the house on Caely where she was born.

Driving through the old neighborhood in summertime was like seeing it as a girl again. For years, the Humphrys only went to Hamtramck for the Ciocias' annual Christmas Eve dinner when all the old buildings were covered with exhaust-stained snow. Passing familiar places like the Kowalski factory on Holbrook, the Conat Theater, and Liberty State Bank revived memories. Ciocia Stas had gone to The Dermaway Beauty School, and Jaja traded at Witkowski's Men's Store.

As she turned onto Caely, June's breathing fluttered. "I'm home."

Ciocia Stas lived alone in the two-story now, and Ciocia Honey and Uncle Pep owned the single level ranch on the adjoining lot.

"Doll?" Honey appeared through the narrow gap separating the two houses.

"Cioc."

Honey scurried forward, a brisk, effervescent walk that refused to acknowledge sixty years of hard physical work. She hugged June. "Where's Pierce?"

"Home."

"You drove all dat way yourself?!"

"Sure."

"I can't believe you're here. Come on in."

June grabbed the lunch meat and followed Honey toward the smaller house. "Can I leave cold cuts in your fridge?"

"I'll take 'em."

"I can."

"I've got two arms. You're my guest."

"Thanks, Cioc."

"Stas'll be back in a minute. She's down da street helping Pani Kashubinska clean house. You know Pani broke her elbow?"

"Her elbow?"

"Split in tree places." She held up three fingers. "She slipped on da grass pushing her lawn mower."

"She still does her own lawn? She's nearly eighty years old."

"Oh, it's okay," Honey led June into the house. "She was in no real danger. It's a manual mower."

"I'll bet she hates not being able to clean on her own."

"She was ironing yesterday wid her left hand." Honey lit a burner on the stove. "Tea?"

"Sure."

"I said, 'Pani, give me dat iron. You'll burn yourself.'"

"'I'll burn in hell for being lazy on such a good day like today,' she said. Den she kept going wid her good hand." Even as Honey spoke her lips pursed into a dimpled smile. As thin as Honey'd been all her life, her hands gripped the kettle heartily.

Honey zigzagged from the cupboard to the table with sugar, napkins, cup and saucer, then to the sink where she arranged paczki and chrusciki on a platter.

"You've had lunch?"

"No."

"You want pierogi?" She rinsed powdered sugar off her fingers.

"No, thanks."

"I made cheese and kapusta just yesterday. Cheese is still your favorite?"

June smiled. She remembered. It was good to be with her family.

"Where's Uncle Pep?"

"The V.F.W. hall. They're setting up for a wedding tonight. You remember Stephan's Italian friend Gino?"

"Sure, with the wavy black hair."

"Yeah. His daughter."

"His daughter? How old is she?"

"Twenty? Twenty-one?"

"Twenty-one!"

"Yeah. Dey're having a big mass at Our Lady, Queen of Apostles, den da reception at da V.F.W."

"The groom's side must be Polish."

"No, he's...dat dere...what you call...Uke—"

"Ukrainian?"

"Yeah, yeah." She laughed. "I always tink Euker so I remember. I tole Gino's mother, 'He's marrying a gambler?' and she just looks at me crazy. She doesn't know what I'm talking about."

"Seems like Hamtramck's got everybody now. Italian, Ukrainian."

"Two Albino families, too."

"Really?"

"Yeah, one down da end of our street. Den across the alley from Stas, a young couple with two littluns."

"Albinos?"

"Yeah."

"Do kids make fun of them?"

"Fun? No, dat dere welcome wagon even brought 'em stuff. You know, bread, salt, traditional Polish stuff, but what else? It's what we know."

"People with no skin color?"

"No," she smiled.

"That's what that is."

"No."

"Yes."

"What?"

"Albinos."

"No," Honey chuckled.

"Yeah, Cioc."

"Oh! Den I mean, um, Albin—? Alban—?"

"Albanians?"

"Yeah, yeah, yeah, Albanians." Honey snickered into her cupped hand. "Albinos."

June laughed with her.

"Things change, eh Cioc?"

"Oh, yeah. But you roll on or get left behind."

June looked around. "So many memories."

"Memories are for ol' people."

"I could live on memories."

"You? You're too young. If you're spending time lookin' at memories, you're not doin' anything to make new ones."

June took comfort in the little details of this house: placemats embroidered with the Lord's Prayer under the glass tabletop, ceramic mushrooms on the wall, the Last Supper print she and Jaja bought years and years ago. "I guess."

"Are you goin' to tell me what happened?"

"Happened?"

"A lie dat you may tell today
In Boza's ear forever stays."

It was a catechism rhyme June hadn't thought of since she was a child. Unlike Ciocia Honey, June had no trace of little girl left in her. Somewhere she had let it go. Perhaps I'll recover it here on Caely, she thought.

"Did he do something?"

"To me?"

"You? Da kids?"

"No. How could he? He's never around."

"He isn't having—"

"An affair? Who, Pierce? Cioc," she scolded, "He can't stop thinking about work enough to be a husband and father. He sure's not gonna waste any energy on some Playboy bunny. Not unless she looks like a hotel toilet."

"Well," Honey shrugged, "He's at dat age when a man begins worrying if he's made good choices."

"You think?"

"Sure. He's 40?"

"Pretty soon."

"Now's da time. He still has a chance to make himself what he probably dreamed about as a kid. Only what he dreamed didn't have tree kids with minds of their own and bills for pediatricians and orthopedics."

"Orthodontists?"

"When a man gets what he wants early, he starts wondering if he asked for da wrong thing. It's not wort anything unless it's tough. He's been looking in his work and thinking he's gonna find something. I bet he just started to figure out there's nothing lasting dere."

"I don't think he's learning anything. Work, work, those damn hotel toilets, now this pool. He's worse than ever."

"He's scareder dan ever. What do you do when you work all your life for something that looks so promising and it turns out empty? You try to fill dat emptiness before you let go of what you know."

"Where does that leave me and the kids?"

"Don't know. What are you learning?"

June hadn't considered that. "I don't understand his dreams. I don't believe in dreams."

"Oh, Doll."

"I don't, Cioc. I haven't since what happened to Stephan."

Honey stared blankly.

"His arm and baseball."

"Oh! Him and dat Charlie Granger."

"Gehringer. He wanted to be the next Charlie Gehringer. He coulda been, too, if it wasn't for Uncle Jan."

"Doll, dat was tirty years ago."

"Point is, I don't understand Pierce's obsession with his dreams."

"And you never will. You don't need to. It's not you."

"Why can't he—?"

"'Cause it's not him."

"Lately that ain't sayin' much."

"Yeah, well," Honey rose from the table, "Dat's why

it's good to have lots of family. When some get on your nerves, you got plenty of others to keep you occupied."

"For how long?"

"You got more strenth than you ever gave yourself credit for."

Strenth. June felt a softening inside. These little uniquenesses — the Polish inflections that sounded like mispronunciations, the squint of Honey's eye when she was sure you were lying — were so warmly familiar. It was like reliving days before Jaja and her mother died.

The side door opened. "Doll?" Ciocia Stas stepped up from the landing.

"Cioc."

"You didn't tell us you were coming."

"I was being spontaneous."

"Pierce in the lilla boys' room?" She glanced toward the hall as she approached the table.

"She came on her own," bragged Honey.

Stas's dark eyebrows rose so high they touched her auburn bangs. "Oh!" she smiled mischievously. Nearing her sixties, she was still a striking woman.

"Did you at least bring a kid?" She approached the table and picked through the chrusciki.

"Nope."

"Good, more for me." She bit off one end and licked powdered sugar off her lips.

"Hon', you outdid yourself."

"I didn't make doze."

"Then you outbought yourself. Either way, you did good."

"Pani any better?"

"Mad as hell at herself for not being able to do, but feisty as ever."

"Can you imagine not being able to do for yourself?" Honey wondered aloud. "What'll you have to drink, Stas? Cream soda or somethin' real?"

"Is June drinking?"

"Doll, you want a shot with Stas and me?"

"No, but you go."

"If we're gonna have drinks, come over to my place. I'll fix us a shot and show you my tufting."

"You're tufting now?"

"Sophie sent me some material of Krakowianka from Poland."

June frowned. Her Polish wasn't what it used to be.

"Dancers in Polish costumes. Come see."

She smiled. "Krakowianka. I remember."

Next door, Stas served drinks and spread two panels on her dining room table. "These are already done."

The old table creaked when June leaned on it to inspect Stas's work. "Such detail."

"I can't take credit for the design, I just did the tufting and matting."

"Still, the overall effect is beautiful."

Honey helped her raise the third panel, three times the size of the others.

"I'm gonna hang this one over here," she glanced at the wall behind her. "And those two will go on your movie star wall."

"My what?"

"I still call it your movie star wall. You had everybody up there, Greta Garbo, Gene Tierney, and...Scarlet O'Hara."

"Vivien Leigh," June recalled.

"Yeah. Remember Pani used to come over and yell at us? 'Whatza matter with you people? You got a family. Whadya need dese up here for?'"

"I put Gloria Swanson's picture up there, too. Ma asked me to."

"I don't remember dat one."

"I didn't leave her up long. Ma told me to add her because she was Polish. But, God the woman frightened me. I was so scared I'd grow up to look like her." She pinched her upper lip. "I used to squeeze this mole because I was afraid it would grow big like the one on her chin. I didn't want that. I wanted to be pretty, like you two."

"See, Doll. You did dream."

"As a kid. When I grew up, I knew what I could get. That's why I got married and had children."

Stas pointed to the wall. "You put a picture of a man up there, too. For a little while."

"Gary Cooper in *Pride of the Yankees*."

"He was good lookin'. You liked him, eh?"

"I put it up for Stephan and his baseball dream."

"Oh, God," Stas cackled, "If I had to hear the name Charlie Gehringer one more time."

"See, I tole you," Honey laughed. "We were just talkin' about dat at my house."

"While the whole world was worrying about Nazis, that cousin of yours was hitting balls of tape into the neighbor's victory garden with a broomstick."

"He was good. If it wasn't for Uncle Jan and his temper, Stephan would have been a champion."

"Jan wasn't always like dat. He came back from da war madder'n hell. He never explained."

"But he took it out on his own boy."

"More than you know," Stas admitted.

"But that one time was unforgivable."

"What got him so riled dat time anyway?"

"The kids lost our ration books!"

"Ooo, yeah. We were all mad at you's."

"Ciocia Stas made us go to the store."

"I was listening to the Gabriel Heater Report and you two were making too much noise. I figured you could make it down the street and back without losing a month's worth of food rations. Ya weren't babies."

"It was an innocent mistake. He shouldn't have beat Stephan like that."

"Did Stephan tell you about his arm that night?"

"No, Cioc. I didn't know till after he told you days later."

"He shoulda said something sooner. By the time we got him to the doctor, the muscles were all damaged."

"He tried to get back him aim. I practiced with him. But he lost his strength. That ball went every place but where he wanted it to go."

"He ended up doing all right for himself."

"But he never was the same after that either. That's what I mean about dreams. You can't trust them."

Stas turned to Honey. "I missed something?"

"June was talkin' to me earlier about Pierce. He works a lot."

"He's no bum. What's the problem?"

"It's been so hard, Cioc. I'm alone all the time. Even with a house full of kids."

Ciocia Honey patted June's hand. "I'll pray for you. You watch. It'll help."

"Thanks, Cioc." June sighed. "I miss you two."

"We're right here."

"We're always here," Stas chuckled. "Especially me. I don't even drive."

"I wish I could just stay here."

"Your old room's still up there. You need to spend the night?"

"No, I want things to be like they were before. I miss Ma and Jaja."

"Pa always said 'If you're spending all your time with memories, you're not making new ones.'"

"I tole you!"

"That's not livin', Doll."

"I'm so lonely."

"Talk to him."

"He's never there. I mean even when he's with me, he's not there."

"Then start small. Talk about lilla things. Then get to what's really going on for you."

"I don't want to fight."

"Don't fight. Talk."

"I'm so mad at him and his silly schemes. We just got this pool and already Mark's friend nearly drowned."

"Is he all right?"

"Yeah."

"Close calls are signs," Honey warned. "Boza's tappin' on your door. Better answer Him."

"How?"

Stas reached for June's hand. "Have the courage to be honest."

"I'm tired, Cioc," June's dam of tears broke. "I'm not an old woman, but I am tired."

"Course you are. Carrying a burden alone is exhausting. Tell him what you're feeling."

"He won't listen."

"When you tell people the truth, they can't help but hear it."

"He won't understand."

"You'd be surprised. He might even agree with you."

"Oh, yeah, he'd take the blame just like that?"

"I didn't say he'd feel responsible, I said he might agree. If you're this miserable with him, he's probably just as miserable with you."

June stopped sniffling. "With me?"

Stas smiled. "When you tell the truth…"

"You think I—?"

"She don' think anythin', Doll. Dat's her point. Unless you tell people the trut', you got no idea what's going on with dem either. Right, Stas?"

"I think so."

"What if I don't know the truth myself?"

"Test it."

"But he'll just—"

"Don't prove it to him. Prove it to yourself."

June wiped the tears from her cheek. "If it doesn't work, I'm coming back."

"Got room for you and anybody you bring with you."

"Doll's a great guest," Honey smiled. "She brings lunch meat."

"You brought lunch meat and you didn't offer me any?" Stas stood.

Honey followed suit. "It's in my fridge."

"Just some ham and salami and a little bologna."

"Then what are we doin' here?" Stas led Honey and June out the door. "It's lunch time."

"I left some egg bread and pumpernickel in the car."

"You got pickles in there, too?"

June laughed. "No, but I have Mary Janes and Squirrels, and Bit-O-Honey."

"Bring 'em. That's dessert!"

From her car, June watched Stas and Honey parade next door. It was good to be home, even for an afternoon.

On his usual trek to Wise Owl Book Shoppe, Mark did-n't feel that familiar enthusiasm well inside him. Scanning the movie tie-in novels left him completely uninspired. The familiar smell of uncut pages didn't even invite him into the escape of reading.

At the magazines, the comfort of crisp pages between his fingertips eluded him.

"'Scuse me," someone passed behind Mark as he

flipped through a Hollywood magazine.

Mark looked up to see who passed. A handsome young man with thick dark hair and a mole on his upper lip captivated him. Behind his magazine, Mark watched him browse the center rack, select a magazine, and start flipping through it.

Comparing himself to the young man, Mark felt less isolated. Here they were, each alone on a summer afternoon, with almost identical mannerisms flipping through copies of...Mark looked at the cover of the young man's magazine: *Sports Illustrated.* He was holding *Rona Barrett's Gossip.*

Embarrassed, Mark moved to the center section to find a less sissified magazine that might interest him. "Excuse me," Mark walked behind him and discovered that politeness was all they had in common. Nothing in the middle rack appealed to Mark at all.

As the young man left, Mark watched his confident gait with envy.

Mark returned to the rack of silver screen magazines, but resuming his search for stars to whom Mark meant nothing made him feel immature and lonely. He left Wise Owl empty-handed and emotionally hungry. Liking some fantasy movie was fine for a kid, he decided, but a guy wouldn't do that. He thought of the young man in the book store and wondered what it would be like to be him.

"I'll change." Mark began by emulating the young man's walk. Instead of feeling strong and confident, Mark felt conspicuous until he resumed his natural stride.

Returning to the court, Mark found his opportunity to

make amends with Amil, who was alone reading his news-paper on his front porch.

Without stopping to plan his words, Mark said, "I'm sorry."

"About what, son?" Amil closed his paper.

"What I said about the party. I really thought my parents were gonna invite all the neighbors."

"I didn't give it a second thought."

"You didn't?"

"Kids are always saying things. It left my mind as soon as I walked away."

Mark felt lonelier than ever.

Driving home from Hamtramck, June wondered how to tell Pierce why she was gone so long. As she waited for her order at the A & W Drive-In, excuses jumbled in her head. By the time she reached the house, she was trembling. Strenth, June reminded herself.

"Boy," Pierce smiled as she entered, "You took the long route today!"

June thought she might hyperventilate just getting the words out. She began unwrapping the foot longs and fries so she didn't have to look at Pierce. "I saw Stas and Honey."

"Where?"

"Caely."

Pierce laughed until he saw June's severity. "You went to the East Side by yourself?"

She looked at Pierce. "I needed to see them." Her voice sounded as though she were speaking into fan blades. "I miss my mother." June heard the words spill out as if they weren't hers. "You're so lucky to still have yours."

Pierce nodded.

June was dumb struck. My mother? That wasn't what I wanted to say at all.

"Did you go to the cemetery?"

"No."

"Do we need to?"

"No."

"We could take a ride there tomorrow. Go to church maybe first, then drive out there after lunch?"

"You don't understand." No, she thought, I don't understand. What am I talking about? Say it, June told herself, tell the truth.

Ideas scrambled until she couldn't formulate a coherent thought. What do I want to say, "I'm angry about the pool"? What good does that do now? "I'm tired of you working so much"? That's a fault?

I knew the problem was just me. Maybe I wasn't clear enough with Ciocia Stas. If I had been, she might have given me different advice. How do I tell the truth when I don't know what it is?

"Understand what?"

As June struggled to express her discontent, a vision of her cosmetic bag crystallized. Showing him that would say what she couldn't. The trembling started again. She began breathing like Mark during an asthma attack.

"June?"

"I can't, Cioc," she said aloud.

"Can't what?"

"I don't know what I'm thinking." She turned away. "You ready for a hot dog?"

Pierce put his arms around her. "Do I need to worry?"

"No, Pierce, I'm fine. I guess being with the ciocias made me sentimental."

"I know what you mean. The other day I was thinking about my mom's old wool sweater. Of all things."

"Imagine that," June pulled free. "Call in the boys, will you? They must be starving."

Even at their informal Saturday meals, the Humphrys ate together at the table.

Nicki waited for her father to say something about Toke.

"How was work?" June asked her.

"I don't mind Saturdays. We close so early, I still have the whole day to do something good."

"What'd you do?"

"Nothing. I don't have a car, remember?"

"Have you talked to your father about when you can get it back?"

"I got a better idea," Nicki told June as if Pierce weren't right there. "I'm saving for a Harley."

June and the boys stopped cold. Tense shouldered, everyone looked at Pierce, preparing themselves for a flying foot long and an abrupt exit.

Pierce's breath didn't whistle and his index finger didn't rub the corner of his mouth raw. He merely paused between bites to say, "When we sell your car, I get half the trade-in. I could use the money."

Nicki didn't know to be furious or relieved. For the first time in their relationship, he genuinely didn't give a damn.

Chapter

15

A weekend of worry didn't brace Pierce for the plummeting spiral that continued the following week. With the job stopped, Holiday Inn was losing money. "If you don't get work started again immediately," the Holiday Inn franchisee threatened, "we'll sue. This work is across state lines. We're talking federal suits."

Hours later, the general contractor called. "This delay is costing us time and money, you damn swindler. Get this job going or I'll sue your conniving ass."

Pierce finally got through to BA Hugh Sloan, who refused to consider his pleas for two days before setting an appointment with Pierce.

"You said yourself, Hugh, you know me. I wasn't the one who messed up. But I'm left to fix it."

"My hands are tied, Pierce. My guys don't care who's to blame. Bottom line, they've been screwed. They don't forget, and they won't let it happen again."

"But I'd be willing to make up for what they lost...in the long run. I'm a small operation—"

"The Morgan Company's small?"

"No, The American Company is. The Morgan Company's not helping me here."

"That doesn't look good."

"That's their point. Because I can't get any proof to pin the responsibility on them, they can absolve themselves of any culpability and leave me to clean up the mess. That's what I'm doing here. You're my only hope."

"But, Pierce, you screwed up big time."

"If I could have prevented this from happening, Hugh, God knows I would have. But it really was beyond me. So I'm left to deal with where I am now."

"What do you have?"

"I could contribute to the Union Welfare Fund. I'd give handsomely over time."

"Well, that's something. What else?"

"I—I don't know that I have anything else to offer up front. All my assets are tied into the modules. If they don't get made and into the Holiday Inn structures, I've got nothing. But if your Union thought of something it wanted, I'll honor anything the best I can."

"Let me talk to the guys. I'll get back to you."

Meanwhile the unraveling continued. Beyond suing for possible loss of final mortgage financing end commitment and loss of income, the hotel developers added to their grievances non-fulfillment of contract, loss of interim of mortgage commitment, delay of opening the hotel, and possible increase of construction costs.

Pierce's only salvation was the Union's response.

Hugh finally called Thursday morning.

"Pierce."

"Yes, Hugh."

"I worked really hard with my guys. And I spoke up for you, really I did."

He sounded so final. "There must be something they're willing to let me do."

"Well there is."

Pierce sat up. "Yes?"

"My tradesmen will consider restarting the job only if they get to complete the work on every module themselves. That includes dismantling all the completed modules and letting them re-plumb those, too."

This wasn't even remotely possible. Some of the modules were in Oshkosh, some in Detroit, others already inserted into the main structure of the Holiday Inn in Pontiac. "Is there anything else they'd consider?"

"I knew it didn't make any sense to use all that time and expense to redo all that work, but that's as far as they'll budge."

"Then I'll work with that, Hugh. Thank you."

Pierce contacted The Morgan Company for one final plea for financial backing. If they had a shred of conscience, they'd relent.

"We would only do that if we were at fault," Lenny Gordon insisted.

"But you are."

"You keep saying that, Pierce. Have you convinced yourself of it yet?"

"Let's not quibble about that. With your backing to cover the rework and delays, we can still complete the job.

And not just this one, remember. This is a national franchise, and Hilton expressed interest, too."

"Pierce."

"Help me, Lenny."

"Even if we could, our help would make us look as guilty as you. The resulting lawsuits that would come to The Morgan Company would cost us, in money and reputation, more than we'd ever gain from your project."

"Lenny."

"We're running a business here, Pierce, not a charity. Beg somebody else."

When she was ready to leave for bowling, June went downstairs to say good-bye to Pierce. He was staring so blankly she cleared her throat before entering to warn him of her presence. "I'm off."

"June."

"Yes?"

He paused. "Is you gas tank full?"

A memory stirred in her. Would he remember too? She repeated words from long ago. "Full, please."

He wasn't paying attention. "Great."

"What's bothering you?"

"Huh?"

"You're somewhere else. You all right?"

"Ooowhh, what a day."

"Lotta work?"

He rubbed the sore on his mouth.

"You can tell me."

"No, it's business."

"Things'll work out. You always make sure they do."

"Just go, have fun. I'll be here when you get home."

"The boys are playing. If they swim later, make them hang their bathing suits on the clothesline before they go to bed."

"Okay."

"Their towels, too. Mark can reach. He'll do it for both of them."

"Um-hm."

"Nicki's going to Pine Knob tonight. You know concerts can last pretty late, and since she's not the one driving..."

"Right, I've got you."

"If you have something on your mind, that's one thing you don't need to worry about tonight."

"Thanks." He gave her the saddest smile she'd ever seen. The image of it stayed with her all the way to Satellite.

As she hopped into his Tempest, Nicki immediately noted Nelson's tension. "'ts goin' on?"

"What do ya mean?"

"Nothin', geez. Candy's coming with us, right?"

"Yeah."

"You usually pick her up first. Lucky me." What an opportunity. She sidled a little closer to Nelson.

"Have you talked to her?"

"Saw her yesterday."

"You's guys got together without me? And I was home."

"How's your friend?"

"Friend? I hang out with you two."

"The Harley guy."

Nicki slid back toward the door. "Harley guy?"

Nelson looked at her.

"Him? He just gives me a ride to work. You know my dad took my car from me."

"You work with this guy?"

"No. He's an artist."

"Then why ask him for a ride instead of me?"

"I would have, but it started after our wreck and you were in no condition—"

"How long you known him?"

"Just awhile." Nicki tried to cover her embarrassment by grinning. "Are you jealous?"

"I'd have to care to be jealous, wouldn't I?"

As she watched Nelson walk up to Candy's front door, Nicki was thrilled. He did care. Her mind spun with possibilities for finally starting something deeper with Nelson. She just had to do it without hurting Candy.

"Hey," Candy slid across the driver's seat, pushing Nicki toward the passenger door.

"That's a cute top. Is it new?"

Candy smiled at Nelson. "Yeah. You like?"

"Enough to borrow it."

"Like it would fit you," Candy giggled.

"Oh, right. I couldn't get one boob in there. You've got

room to spare."

Rather than retaliating with another barb, Candy took Nelson's hand and held it until they arrived at the Big Boy on Telegraph Road. Nicki didn't say another word. In the restaurant, Candy and Nelson sat on one side of the booth, leaving Nicki to face them from the other.

As she sat down, Nicki's heart sunk. Fran Davenport was with her mom and little brother in the next booth. Her friendship with Fran had been the painful turning point that compelled her to change from Veronica to Nicki. The summer between sixth and seventh grade, they spent every day together swapping clothes, earning Girl Scout badges, and playing Easy Money with rules they changed at whim.

Back in school, Nicki felt stabbed when Fran not only ignored her, but made friends with Erin and Lisa, two girls they both hated. Over Christmas break, Fran called her. "You're my favorite friend," she said, and Nicki gullibly gave her another chance.

Fran's second slash left scars. In the spring, Nicki joined the school softball league, as had Fran and Erin and Lisa. For one tournament, Sister Bernadette made Fran and Lisa team captains. As the best player in school, Fran was always selected. But Lisa was chosen only because Carol, the school's other star female athlete, was absent. After Fran won the toss to begin picking her teammates, Nicki was surprised at her hesitation over first choice. Fran darted her eyes back and forth between Erin and her.

"Veronica," Fran pointed to her first choice.

Nicki was elated. She had held out hope for her friendship with Fran. In front of Erin and Lisa and the entire seventh grade class, Fran chose Nicki.

Fran's next pick surprised Nicki. She selected Deana Zewicki, the fattest, most uncoordinated girl in the league. She couldn't even run to first base without wheezing.

Fran's third choice was no better. By the time both teams were selected, Nicki realized she and Fran were the only good players on their team.

"With the two of us, we can pull this off," Nicki told Fran as they headed onto the field.

"Oh, I plan to pull something off," Fran replied. "We'll be out of this tournament after the first game. If I can't play with Lisa and Erin, I don't want to play at all. Why do you think I picked you?"

Nicki was determined to make the most of this opportunity at Big Boy. With Fran clearly in earshot, Nicki could prove once and for all that vulnerable Veronica Lynn Humphry was dead. "I was in my room," she spoke a little louder than usual, "When I just sensed something was wrong. I have that ability now." Nelson and Candy were attentive.

"I couldn't have heard anything because I had the stereo so loud. But I knew something was happening, so I went to find out what it was. When I didn't hear Brandon screaming in the kitchen, which is what he does every time he gets hurt, I looked out front to see if he fell off his bike or something. Nobody there either.

"So I rushed to the patio door and there were people from all over the neighborhood standing in this huge group beside our pool."

Fran looked back briefly and saw Nicki.

Nicki ignored her. "I pushed my way through the crowd and Mark's friend was laying there not breathing while my ma and a neighbor guy were trying to bring him back."

"No way."

"Yeah. But they didn't know what the hell they were doing 'cause he wasn't moving. They were trying to breathe into his mouth, but they didn't even tilt his head back."

"Man alive, what'd you do?"

"I just plowed right through and saved his life."

"No."

"I knew what to do."

"Were you nervous?"

"No, I was too hung over."

They all laughed. "God only knows how much we drank the night before. I knew what to do, and I did it. The coolest thing: Yesterday the kid came to our house and thanked me for saving his life."

"You really did that?" Nelson smiled.

"I came a long way since Girl Scouts, eh?"

"That's bomb."

Telling her story was satisfying. So was sitting here with friends while Fran was stuck with her mom and a brother making mounds of chocolate milk bubbles.

After his last bite of Brawny Lad, Nelson balled up his napkin and belched. His eyes shot toward Candy. "Sorry."

Candy nodded. "That's better."

Following Nelson and Candy toward the exit, Nicki walked past Fran's table and snubbed her.

"Veronica?" Mrs. Davenport squealed.

"Hello, Mrs. Davenport."

"How is your gargantuan pool?"

"It's great!"

"What a catastrophe. First that flood, then Brandon's disappearance. I bet your mother hates the trauma of it all. I know I would."

"She never says."

"Frannie, aren't you going to say hello?"

"Hey, Veronica."

"It's Nicki. I go by Nicki now."

"I bet you two miss the old days. Playing Monopoly all summer long."

"It was Easy Money, Mother."

Nicki shook her head. "I don't remember."

"Oh, come now. You couldn't possibly forget a whole summer. That's all you girls did. Aren't childhood friends wonderful?" she beamed. "What ever happened to you two? Just because you go to different schools now doesn't mean you can't be friends. We're back yard neighbors, for goodness sakes. You ought to come over again some time, Vero—, Nicki."

"Mother."

"Oh, Frannie, instead of being boy crazy, you should cherish your friendships." She turned to Nicki. "My girlhood friends and I meet for dinner every month, religiously. I wouldn't trade the experience for a date with Clark Gable."

"He's dead, Mother."

She giggled. "You know what I mean. Frannie, the time

to cultivate friendships is now before you're dating anyone."

Through the window to the parking lot, Nelson waved
at Nicki and pointed to his car. "I'm dating," Nicki said.
"Did you see him leave?"

"That boy who passed? Very Burt Lancaster! But was-
n't he with—?"

"She's a friend. I wouldn't drop my best friend just
because I started dating someone. What kind of person
would do that?" Nicki inched away from their table. "Gotta
go."

"Good-bye then. Tell your mother I hope she's coping
with her monstrosity."

Nicki felt victorious until she joined Nelson and Candy
in the car. They didn't stop kissing until after Nicki
slammed her door. This was going to be a long night.

Chapter

16

Everything Mark cared about—his time with Russell, his passion for Amil, his obsession with *The Poseidon Adventure*—was ebbing, and he had no idea how to stop it. Ignoring his dad's rule about not swimming alone, he dove into the pool so hard the impact stung. He unhooked the divider rope and swam the length of the pool until he couldn't catch his breath.

"What are you doing?" Brandon stepped to the edge of the shallow end holding a shovel and a Hot Wheels car.

Mark shrugged.

"Can I swim, too?"

"I didn't even ask if I could come in."

"So?"

"I don't want you to get in trouble."

"I still want to swim."

"Where have you been? There's gravel stuck to your knees."

"I made a city out of the dirt by the fence. Wanna see?"

"I thought you wanted to swim."

"Oh, yeah. Will you watch me if I do?"

"Get your suit on, and let Dad know we're out here." By the time Brandon returned, Mark forgot to ask him if he'd told Dad where they were.

"I'm gonna jump," Brandon warned in mid-air. In the shallow end he spit water and hopped up and down with his eyes closed.

"You need your life jacket?"

"I'm not a baby. Come down here. Let's play Commando."

"Commando?"

"You know how?"

"Yeah."

"Will ya?"

"Sure."

Brandon dog paddled to the side of the pool. "Go over there," he pointed. "Turn around and keep your eyes closed."

Crossing the pool, Brandon paused after every splash. Though Mark could distinguish Brandon's entire trek, he never yelled "Target detected." Letting his kid brother win pleased him. It was even more satisfying when he saw Brandon's glee at game's end.

"I'm good, huh?"

"You're really good."

"I thought you woulda heard me, there," he pointed toward the middle of the pool as if he could recall the exact spot, "'cause I a'most slipped and my nose went under water. But I didn't even blow air out, did I?"

"No."

"I held my nose, but didn't make any noise with it."

"None."

"Let's play again."

And they did.

In his basement office, Pierce had nothing left to do. The American Company was already receding into the past. Its brief existence punctuated a powerful twenty year build-up that would shred over the next few months.

The sharp ring of his telephone jolted Pierce to the present. His heart raced. *My last-second miracle?* Pierce hoped. He took a deep breath before picking up the receiver.

"Hello."

"Hull-o, Pierce." It was unmistakably Ed Manduski.

"Ed," Pierce died a little all over again.

"Pierce, I d-don't mean to pry," he pulled the words from his mouth like taffy, "But I heard a rumor. About the company?"

"What rumor was that, Ed?"

"Are we closing?"

Pierce didn't know what to say. He knew the answer, but Ed depended on Pierce for his income and the little emotional balance his job provided. How could he tell him the truth? How could he lie either?

"Pie-erce, are you there?"

"Yes, Ed. It's true." *There, I've said it.* "But I'll take care of you. I promise to make the transition as easy as possible."

"Pie-erce?"

"Yes, Ed?"

"But Pierce."

"I'll keep my word. Count on it."

When Pierce hung up he had no idea how to deliver on his promise. Nothing came to him: no idea, no instant solution, none of the ingenious strategies for which he was so often praised.

Suffocating in his little cubby hole of an office, Pierce moved into the basement family room defined by a huge gold area rug. He noticed veins in the floor and pulled up one corner of the rug to check the foundation. Instead of cracks, he discovered faint scribbles in colored chalk that Nicki had sketched when she was little.

They revived painful memories. Pierce thought the drawings were not only insignificant, but also pretty darned creative. But June was so upset, Pierce scolded Nicki until she cried.

Pierce sat on the floor trying to remember what Nicki had drawn back then. The faded pastel streaks were interrupted by sweeping white scratches made later by Mark's roller skates.

Pierce was initially glad when Mark skated in the basement without interrupting his work. But when he looked up and noticed Mark's swagger as he pushed off with his skate, Pierce went to Big Bill's Sporting Goods and bought Mark a baseball glove. Despite Mark's vehement objections, Pierce took him to the front yard to play catch.

"Watch the ball," Pierce repeated as Mark kept running to the neighbor's yard to retrieve missed catches. "Keep your eye on the ball, not your glove."

Pierce knew Mark was more defiant than uncoordinated. Mark never took instruction well from him. Rather than force Mark to learn from him, Pierce signed Mark up for league play with the best of intentions. Playing a sport would give Mark the confidence he lacked around other boys. He would learn teamwork and experience a sense of belonging. That was Pierce's hope. Instead, Mark found only humiliation.

Watching Mark's games was excruciating. "Come on, son," Pierce whispered to himself on that last awful day when Mark came up to bat. "Knock that ball outa here."

With his first ferocious attempt, Mark's bat whisked several inches over the top of the ball and missed it completely. Pierce winced.

"It's okay, Mark. You're trying too hard," Pierce hollered. He could see Mark's shoulders stiffen. "You can do it, son. Easy does it."

Mark dug his foot into the ground, swung wildly, and smacked the tee. It bent forward and spit the ball on the ground with a heavy "thup."

Pierce took a nervous breath. Instead of shouting any encouragement, he prayed. "Let him get a hit. A little one. Let him know he can do something."

More fiercely than ever, Mark cocked the brim of his cap and swung with such might it spun him around. The bat breezed over the ball close enough for the wind to push it off the tee for a third strike.

Pierce watched Mark's reaction. Unlike the boy before him who struck out, Mark wasn't crying. While relieved that Mark wasn't in the dugout making a scene, Pierce could not comprehend how Mark could be unaffected by such public humiliation.

Pierce released the corner of the basement rug. *How am I going to get us all through this alone?*

After bowling her frame, Doris plopped beside June. "I'm exhausted. All I did this week was pick up after five kids."

"I thought you had four?"

"Don is still laid off. He makes five. I'm so ready for him to go back to work so I can have some quiet and watch my story."

"Your story?"

"*All My Children.* I don't even know what's going on."

"I don't follow soap operas," Evelyn confessed. "They upset me."

"That rubbish?"

"What's the matter, Helen, can't follow the story lines?"

"Follow 'em? I could write 'em. Even better, I could end every soap opera with one episode." She tossed the ball down the lane.

"Yeah?"

"They're nothing but people lying and keeping secrets when they know they shouldn't. If everybody was honest with everybody else, there wouldn't be any story left."

"Oh that would do it? Everybody could just be honest?"

"When you tell the truth, people know where you stand. If they have any backbone at all, they'll be honest with you, too."

"What if they don't have backbone?"

"They'd get it if enough other people showed some. One person could start a chain reaction of telling the truth, and the show would be over in half an hour."

"Happily ever after, eh?"

"I said I'd make the show honest, not stupid. Being truthful doesn't make you happy, or popular, but it makes you clear. I always know what I like and what I don't."

"I'll say."

"And I have a pretty good idea when people like me and when they don't."

Evelyn took her turn on the lane. "We like you, Helen."

"Oh, be real. Not always. Sometimes I get on your nerves."

"Sometimes?" Doris laughed.

"Well, you are a bit bossy."

"And sometimes you're daft. But I tell you to your face. Just like I tell Doris she's not the queen of Sheba that she thinks she is, and June that..."

June perched in her seat.

"Watch yourself, Helen," Doris growled. "June's my friend now. I'll take care of her."

"I'm her neighbor. She knows me better than she knows you. I like you, June."

"But?"

"But nothing. I like you, even without a backbone."

"For Chrissakes, Helen, you can be—"

"No," June grabbed Doris' arm. "That doesn't hurt me."

"I told you. She knows she doesn't have a backbone."

"No, Helen. I never showed it to you. You have no idea what I'm made of, and I don't have a thing to prove, to you of all people."

Helen pointed triumphantly. "I knew you had one."

"I'll be damned," Doris grinned at June. "Go knock the hell outa those pins. We need a strike."

Outside Pine Knob Amphitheater, Candy stashed Nelson's bottle of gin in her purse while Nicki checked to see if she had the tickets. Nelson grabbed a blanket, pillows and, at the last minute, a gift-wrapped box.

"What's that?" Candy purred.

"Just something."

She smiled bashfully. "What is it?"

"What's what?"

"In there. Is that for me?"

"I don't know what you mean."

She tilted her head and cooed, "Widdow me?"

Oh gawd, thought Nicki.

On the hill with their blanket spread and shoes off, Candy turned toward Nelson and raised her eyebrows pleadingly.

"What?" Nelson asked.

Nicki could feel herself ready to burst out with "All

211

right a'ready, give her the goddam present!" when Nelson
handed Candy the box.

She slid her fingernail under the fold to unwrap the gift
then handed the untorn paper to Nelson.

What's she planning to do, save the paper? thought
Nicki.

"Don't wad that up," Candy warned. "I want to save a
piece of it for my memory book."

Pa-leez, Nicki turned away.

Inside the box was a note that read, "You wear it well."
Inside was a denim jacket with sequined decals down both
arms, and a huge multi-colored heart on the back. In one
pocket were two concert tickets.

Candy screeched. "Tickets to Rod!" She kissed Nelson
again and again.

Rod? The three of them had already planned to attend
the Stewart concert together. Nicki fanned out the tickets.
There were definitely only two. She couldn't even look at
Nelson. She lay on her stomach and pressed her chin deep
into a pillow so her mouth was completely covered. She
had nothing to say.

Throughout the concert, Nicki wanted to escape.
Though Joni Mitchell's melodies were soothing, her lyrics
beat between Nicki's temples. *"Oh I hate you some, I hate you
some, I love you some."* Nicki's sadness was strangling. Later
in the evening, "Help Me" started.

"Didn't it feel good," the speakers chided from every
angle of the amphitheater. "Didn't it feel good" the words
slithered like warm fingers over Nicki.

I want to go home, she thought.

It was already dark when the boys finished swimming. By then they were tired and hungry. Leaving the pool with Brandon, Mark saw light coming through the basement window. "We better be quiet. Dad's still downstairs working."

Once in their pajamas, they sneaked a carton of Sealtest ice cream saturated with Bosco into their room and turned on the black and white Silvertone. Before they reached the bottom of the carton, Brandon wrapped his arms around his stomach. "I ate too much."

Mark turned off the TV and tucked Brandon into bed.

"It hurts."

"You'll be okay. Rest."

"Get Dad."

"And tell him we ate a whole thing of ice cream? He'll be mad." Mark felt a pang of guilt for lying. He knew, for all his absence and indifference, Dad was never mad at them when they were sick. In fact, when Mark was Brandon's age and Mom was staying with their ailing babka, Mark once faked being sick so his father would sit beside him until he fell asleep.

Mark gently rubbed Brandon's belly. "It's all right," he mimicked his father's calming reassurances. "I'm right here. I'll take care of you."

When Brandon moaned, Mark assured, "Shh. It's okay. Rest now."

Mark stayed with him until Brandon drifted off. He

turned off the light and headed to the basement. Mark was surprised to see his father sitting on the area rug. "Dad?"

"Mark."

"You still working?"

"Thinking. I've got some decisions to make. Something wrong?"

Mark felt anxious. "No. Brandon's asleep, and I'm, uh, kinda tired myself. So," his fingers drummed against his leg, "I came to say good night."

"Thank you, son," his dad smiled. "Good night."

Mark nodded, pleased that he had done a good thing. "Good night," he headed up the stairs.

To save his dad the trouble, Mark locked both the back and front doors, turned off the lights throughout the upstairs, then went to bed.

Nicki had little to say all the way home.

"What's got you?" Nelson asked.

As if you don't know. "Nothing."

"This is a cool thing. Be happy for us." He kissed Candy's knuckle.

"We're all still friends, Nicki."

"I know." Nicki was relieved when they finally dropped her off at home. "See ya," she nearly lost her purse slamming the door.

Ascending the porch steps, she found it odd that all the interior lights were already off. She was home early.

Nicki nearly bruised her shoulder trying to push open

the front door. It was locked.

The memory of her father's voice echoed in her head. "Next time I don't unlock. Next time I don't unlock. Next time..."

Nicki was too outraged to even scream. She dug the extra set of car keys from her purse and tore out of the driveway in her Plymouth Fury. Roaring down Beech Daly, Nicki never considered that Toke might not be home. But after pounding on his door, she was afraid that she'd find him with the woman from the photographs.

Toke opened the door. "Hey." With his tousled hair and bleary eyes, he was as accessible as she'd ever seen him.

"Is it all right that I came?"

"Yeah." He stepped back. "I musta drifted off."

Nicki followed Toke to the couch. The familiar sound of Neil Young in stereo comforted her. She burrowed her face into Toke's chest and squeezed him hard.

"Hey, hey, what is it?" His tender voice touched the piece inside of her that she feared had become unreachable. Nicki pressed her lips onto his.

When she stopped, he smiled curiously.

Taking him by the hand, she led him to his bedroom.

"Are you sure?"

She sat on the bed.

He hesitated. Then rather than move toward her, he staggered to his dresser. Nicki felt an emotional vacuum devouring her.

He's going to pull out those pictures and tell me about that woman. No wonder he was so cool about me saying no all the time. He never wanted me. He has her.

But Toke didn't bring her pictures. He held a little tube and something that crackled and smelled like Playtex gloves. Then he closed the door and turned off the light.

Nicki lay back, nervous but relieved. In the darkness, her other senses made up for what she could not see. Muffled lyrics from the other room faded in and out of Nicki's awareness as Toke made love to her.

". . . yellow moon...rise..."

Toke's chest held the faint scent of sweat from when he slept.

". . . across the sky..."

His hair brushed against her face as he hung his head low to kiss her. "You okay?" he whispered.

"Yes." Adjusting to a faint light from a high, small window across the room, Nicki's eyes distinguished only Toke's silhouette. As he bobbed with rhythmic thrusts that sometimes pained her, he looked unreal. In the safety of his shadow, Nicki waited, tense and uncomfortable, until finally Toke arched his back and moaned.

He dropped beside her. She heard a snap like a rubber band before he pulled her to him. "You all right?"

Believing that she had recovered some lost connection she needed back so desperately, Nicki's heart fluttered with nervous anticipation. Then she said it. "I love you."

"What?"

Nicki's body stiffened as she listened, horrified.

"I'm sorry," he tried to restrain his chuckles. "I'm just a little high."

Nicki lay there in silence, wondering how to escape this nightmare. When Toke finally began to snore, she slithered out of his bed and headed home.

After June's declaration, a new confidence shot her scores from 128 and 134 to 176. But the adrenaline that energized her game turned to fear as she drove home alone. In order to truly believe what she told Helen, June had to prove it to herself. The thought terrified her.

She didn't even have to wonder how. Immediately, the image of her cosmetic case flashed through her mind. Once again, June teetered at the edge of the gulf between blackness and hope. Fear coursed through her.

"Tell the trut'," Honey suggested.

Confessing to Pierce that she'd considered running away mortified her. What kind of mother would leave her kids? *But I didn't,* June reassured herself. *I thought about, I packed a bag, but I didn't leave.*

If I put everything away and put the bag back, I haven't hurt anyone. "Okay, I'll do that."

When she pulled into the drive, June was surprised to see Nicki's car gone. *Maybe she and Pierce smoothed things out,* June hoped. *Things seemed to be falling into place on their own.*

June had to use her house key to get in. When she found Pierce and the boys asleep, she seized the opportunity to sneak her cosmetic case into the house. As she closed the front door behind her, she heard Nicki's car pull into the drive. Panicked, June tossed the case into the hall closet and raced to her room. At the last second, she grabbed her nightgown and scurried to the bathroom to get ready for bed.

Nicki arrived home desperate to scrub away her encounter with Toke. Seeing her mom's car and a light from the bathroom window eased Nicki's concern about still being locked out. She braced herself for her father's wrath and pushed open the front door. She paused. Dad was nowhere in the hall. Nicki took shelter in her room until the bathroom was free.

"Nicki?" her mother whispered outside her door.

"I'm home."

"Are you all right in there?"

Her mother's sweet intonation brought tears to her eyes. "I'm real tired, Mom."

"Rest, Nicki."

"G'night."

"Good night."

In the shower, Nicki's mind railed. I'm so tired of giving and getting nothing back. I spent more than $500 on that bastard, and all I have are a few scraps of ugly jewelry I painted myself. I was good to Nelson, and now he takes up with Candy. And my own dad. I trusted him and he reads my diary and takes away my car.

Oh, Gawd. I made love to Toke and he was only high. I told him I loved him. I'm such an idiot! I gave everything and —. Nicki stopped in mid-thought.

You liar, she told herself, remembering the image of

Toke's shadow hovering over her. Making love to Toke's silhouette was the same as finding those pictures in his drawer that night and not saying anything. It was like realizing how she felt about Nelson and keeping silent until it was too late. It was like punishing her father by coming home late instead of telling him how violated she felt by his mistrust.

Being honest with herself was more cleansing than the shower. Nicki returned to her room planning to record her new feelings in Leda, but she couldn't do it. Leda was filled with retaliatory lies meant for her father. She wasn't the pure friend she'd started out being. Convinced there was nothing secret, or valuable, about her any more, Nicki tossed Leda on the vanity and went to sleep wishing this day had never happened.

Chapter

17

Instead of going to Wise Owl on Saturday to add to his *Poseidon Adventure* collection, Mark stowed away his gossip magazines and crammed his novels beside other paperbacks in his dad's bookcase. To squeeze in all his books together, Mark had to pull out one of the other paperbacks already there. The title *Mythology* caught his eye. He pulled it out intending to look up the god Poseidon, but was more intrigued by the muscular, nearly naked young man on the cover. Mark flipped through the pages looking for similar illustrations, but was disappointed to find almost every handsome god looking longingly at a beautiful female.

On a page captioned "The Minotaur in the Labyrinth" Mark was curious about the young man at the entrance of a maze staring at a half-man, half-bull. Mark read Theseus' story. One line in particular excited him. "When Hercules…determined to kill himself, Theseus alone stood by him. Hercules' other friends fled,…but Theseus gave him his hand, roused his courage, told him to die would be a coward's act, and took him to Athens."

Imagining such closeness between men thrilled Mark. That's what I want, he admitted. Fear and withdrawal gave way to nervous hope.

"What you got there, Mark?" Pierce entered his office.

"I found this book of Nicki's about gods and heroes. I'm gonna read it."

"Heroes are good things to have, son. I could use one even now." After Mark left, Pierce made one last effort to salvage his dream. He called his lawyer.

"Is there any way to get the money the Union needs to rebuild the modules?"

"Your only resource is The Morgan Company," Seymour offered, "but even if you sued them, the cost of going to trial, and the appeals even if we won the case, would never get you the resources the Unions want to finish the job."

"That's it then?"

"Pierce, I admire your fortitude, but we've been through this discussion. There is nothing else you can do."

Pierce saved his integrity the only way he knew how. He set a new goal.

Somehow, he thought, I'll repay every debt The American Company incurs throughout the legal battles to come. My company will die with dignity. In time it'll be remembered for its grand potential, and for accepting its fate without shame.

Although he had to do it alone, Pierce determined to

make good on this promise. He was a man of his word.

But after I honor every commitment and close The American Company doors for the last time, what'll be left of me? he worried. Who am I, if not what I've dreamed? He had no idea.

All morning, June watched for an opportunity to retrieve her cosmetic case, unpack, and return it to the basement closet without getting caught. Finally, the house seemed clear. Nicki was in her room, Brandon was outside, and Pierce and Mark were both downstairs.

June pulled the case from the hall closet and sprinted to her bedroom.

—Ring—

June jolted. "Oh, the phone!" She tossed the case in the closet.

"Yes," she barked into the receiver.

"Mrs. Humphry? This is Russell. Is Mark there?"

"Russell," she caught her breath. "Are you feeling all right?"

"Yes, thank you."

"We haven't seen you here much lately. You know you're always welcome."

"Thank you."

"I'll get Mark."

Mark was still holding the Mythology book when he took the call in the kitchen. "Hullo?"

"Mark. It's me."

Russell could never be my Theseus, Mark knew. I don't want that kind of friendship with him.

"I didn't hear from you in a while," Russell continued. "I wasn't gonna call 'cause you owe me an apology."

Mark knew he was right, but it was hard to hear it put so bluntly.

"But with school starting soon I felt like talking to somebody. I'm nervous," he admitted. "I figured you would understand."

Though it was sometimes disarming, Russell's openness empowered Mark. "I am sorry I left like that," he admitted. "I don't know why I did it."

"It's because you're scared."

Panic coursed through Mark. Do you know about me? Did I show some sign even before I figured it out myself? Clutching the receiver, Mark's fingers surged to the beat of his racing heart.

"I know you're afraid of going to D.C., especially now that I'm not going, too."

Mark exhaled. Oh that, he thought.

"But that's why I'm calling you. I'm feeling the same way. I don't know anybody at Crestwood, least not anybody I like."

"Can't you do anything to get back into D.C.?"

"I can't avoid going to Crestwood any more than I can force myself not to be afraid. For now, it's the way it is."

"How's everything so simple for you?"

"It's not simple, it's just obvious. I'm smart like my father. He told me never to lie to myself 'cause then I'll get confused. 'Confused people aren't happy,' he always says, 'and all everybody wants is to be happy.' My dad's a smart guy. I'm getting to be just like him."

"So what do you do when you feel so scared?" Mark asked, hoping for some profound insight he'd never considered.

"I'm doing it," Russell said.

After spending the previous day angry at Nelson and Candy and especially Toke, Nicki woke on Saturday ready to think about something else.

Nicki passed Mark on the way to the kitchen. "My *Mythology* book. Where'd you find it?"

"Dad's office."

"Lemme see."

"I wanted to read it."

"You can, but let me look at it first. I'll give it you after I eat breakfast."

While waiting for her toast to pop up, Nicki couldn't believe the book included only two brief references to Leda. In both, she was only important for giving birth to children who brought either love or war.

"Then who'd I mean to name my diary after?"

Nicki flipped through the first chapter. "Here it is. Athena sprang from Zeus' head." She read, "No mother bore her...fierce and ruthless...Goddess of the City...She was Zeus' favorite child."

All this time, I had it wrong, she thought.

"Morning, Nick," her mom lit the burner under her tea

kettle.

"Mom, you know about mythology?"

"No."

"You know Zeus and Poseidon and Helen of Troy?"

"Poseidon? Ask Mark, he'll know."

"I was wondering about Leda. Do you remember her?"

"'Leda and the Swan,' I heard of that. Wasn't it a poem?"

"No, this is mythology. You know, Greek gods and goddesses, Mount Olympus."

"I guess not then."

"Oh, well, never mind," Nicki headed back to her room.

When Pierce stepped into the kitchen, June was at the table dunking a much-used tea bag into her cup. How often she had done this and never complained. Remorse flushed through him. He never provided for her as he wanted, and now he didn't know if he ever would.

"You're ready for a break so early?"

It had been so long since Pierce really looked at her and was awake to her beauty. Her skin was soft and flawless as still water, punctuated by a pale mole that drew attention to her perfect lips. Even greater than her features, her real beauty came from being more present and vibrant than anyone Pierce ever knew.

He loved her courage. Even though she didn't understand his dreams, she supported them by giving him free reign to follow them. She does that for me, Pierce thought. He wanted to share with her everything he was now going through, but he couldn't find the courage to tell her of his defeat. That would be risking too much. He could survive losing everything else. Losing her would be more than he could bear.

"Pierce?"

Smoldering in his emotions, he rushed past her, saying nothing.

As he shut the door to their bedroom, Pierce felt his heart rupturing. His breathing became thick.

I'm killing myself, he decided. I'm literally worrying myself to death, and there's no one to save me.

He tore off his clothes and pulled on swim trunks.

"Pierce?" June entered just as he was about to open the closet door. "Pierce!"

He turned to her blindly.

"What're you doing?"

He looked at the clothes bundled in his arms. "I was putting these away."

June yanked them from him. "I'll do it. You go swim."

Instead of moving, he studied her face.

"Pierce, what's wrong with you?"

He paused. "June." His next word was eclipsed by a blare of music from Nicki's bedroom.

"What is it?"

Courage had escaped him. "It's nothing."

"Go on then," she shooed him toward the door. "A swim will refresh you. And take off your watch."

Pierce tossed his Timex so hard into the leather jewelry

case, the metal band ripped the lining. He thought of Nicki's jewelry box and the diary key he deliberately replaced at an angle so she would know he'd been reading her diary. What a cowardly thing to do, he thought.

Though he couldn't tell June the truth of his failure, he was determined to set something right. He pulled out Nicki's car keys and knocked on her bedroom door.

"Nicki? Nicki, it's Dad."

Nicki sat up in bed. "Dad?"

"May I come in?"

She turned down the stereo and opened the door. "What is —? You all right? You look sick."

"Nicki," he sat on her bed and patted the mattress. "Come here." Pierce struggled to express his thoughts. Once he began, his directness gave him strength. "It was me reading your diary. I shouldn't have. I'm your father, and you should be able to trust me. I want to trust you, too, but I never gave you much of a chance. Instead I acted behind your back. That's a horrible, horrible thing to do, especially to an honorable person. I'm sorry."

Pierce held her.

Nicki didn't know what to make of her father's strange behavior. She just kept thinking, *Why are you telling me this now? Why didn't say something earlier? Why didn't you talk to me the other night instead of locking me out? Why didn't you say something to me before I —?*

When he hugged her, Nicki's mind stopped racing. His

rhythmic breathing rocked her. Gradually, her rigid back relaxed. Finally she reciprocated.

After a moment, he released her and jingled her keys. "I'd like to start again. Your car, same curfew, no silent treatment, no diary reading."

Nicki took the keys. "Deal."

"But, I'm concerned about some of the things I read, Nicki. I want to talk about them."

"Don't worry," she slid Leda off her dresser and tossed her in the wastebasket. "The new stuff was all lies."

"Is there anything I need to know, Nicki?"

She pictured Toke's silhouette. "No, Dad. We're cool."

Pierce was so affirmed by his successful encounter with Nicki that he stepped up to June at the kitchen sink and kissed her neck.

She yelped. "I thought you were swimming."

"Join me."

"I'm in the middle—" She looked down at the sink full of breakfast dishes. "Sure. I'll let these soak." He followed her to the bedroom.

"Pierce, you don't need to be here when I change."

Sitting at the foot of their bed, he couldn't stop watching her. She pulled her bathing suit from a dresser drawer and modestly changed with her back to him. Her skin shone angelic from light beaming in through the window behind them. He wanted to make love to her right then. Pierce moaned, half from pain, half from desire.

"Can you tell me what's going on now?" she asked.

He pulled her toward him and pressed his cheek against her stomach. He squeezed and would not let go.

"What is it?" her voice was gentle.

"Nothing," the lie fizzled in his mouth like acid.

I can't do this to her. I won't make her suffer for my mistake.

"Pierce."

He wanted to tell her, but couldn't. It would be too cruel.

"Share it with me."

"I've lost the business, June. It's going under."

She said nothing, just cradled his head.

He couldn't look up and face her reaction. "It's not my fault, I did everything honestly. But some people from the Morgan Company...I trusted too much."

"What does this mean?"

"We won't go hungry, and we won't ever lose the house. I promise you that. I promise."

"Yes. You promise."

"But it'll be hard for awhile. Until I get us back on our feet. There may even be—" He was going to mention the lawsuits, but that could come later. That would come later. Now that he began the truth he must come to share it all. In time. If she's willing to hear it. "Are you with me, June?"

She waited so long to reply, fear scaled his stomach and clawed at his throat.

Finally she released him and opened the closet door. She set her avocado make-up case on the bed and was trembling so hard, she could barely release the latches.

She lifted the lid, and methodically pulled out a pair of shorts, a blouse, nightgown and tennis shoes. Without ever looking at Pierce, she replaced all her clothes neatly in their respective drawers. Then she returned to the case and handed Pierce her glass bank of silver pennies.

"Comfy, honey?" she asked.

Her words triggered a memory for Pierce. Snuggling in the front seat of his snow-covered '49 Ford, they had formulated a brief exchange that became the emblem of their falling in love.

"Comfy, honey?" he had asked.

"'Bout to freeze."

"Want my coat?"

"Just the sleeves."

"Full or empty?"

"Full, please."

"Comfy, honey?"

"Mmmm."

When he looked at June now, he was too overwhelmed to speak. In response, he could only whisper, "Mmmm."

After they were composed again, June suggested the whole family swim together. Pierce liked the idea.

"Nicki, Dad again."

"Yeah?"

He peered in. He hadn't noticed earlier how much her room looked as though someone had turned it upside down and let everything fall where it may. Mark would like that image.

"Everybody's going out to swim. Wanna come with us?"

"Everybody?"

"Yep."

"Even Mom? Yeah, I'll go."

Putting on his bathing suit, Mark decided not to re-enact *The Poseidon Adventure*'s underwater scenes when he got to the pool. He was ready for something different. Reading about gods and heroes and fantastic creatures inspired him to seek adventures of his own. Anything seemed possible.

On his way to the pool, Mark saw Amil Nerus struggling with his manual edger. He didn't understand the mix of emotions that stirred inside him because of this man. They made him a little fearful and lonely. But if he were to be totally truthful, they also intrigued and excited him.

If Russell ever faced something so confusing, Mark thought, he would have some answers already. Mark had no answers, only questions. But he was convinced they would lead him out of the fear and loneliness. That's all he knew, and it wasn't much to go on. But it was what he had right now. It was a place from which to start.

When June finally entered the back yard carrying her

camera, the rest of the family was already in the pool.

Pierce was sitting at the edge of the deep end tossing a ball with psychedelic swirls to Brandon.

"Keep your eye on the ball, son," he instructed. "Hold out your hands and watch the ball come toward you. It'll pop right into them."

"My hands are wet," argued Brandon.

"You're right," Pierce agreed. "I'll buy you a mitt and we can practice throwing a baseball in the yard. You'll get what I mean."

Brandon ran off the diving board and caught Pierce's pass in mid-air.

In the shallow end, Nicki leaned over an inflated swan counting Mark's underwater laps.

Rather than take pictures of Pierce and the kids enjoying the water, June set the camera aside and got in the pool herself.

After three lengths, Mark came up for air and was surprised to see his mother in the water.

"Mom," he panted, "You're in. Feels good, doesn't it?"

She agreed. It did.